STEALING GANYMEDE

STEALING GANYMEDE

A NOVEL BY J. WARREN

Rebel Satori Press
Acadia

Published by Rebel Satori Press

For information regarding permission to reprint material from this book, please mail or fax the publisher at the address below or email publisher@rebelsatori.com.

Rebel Satori Press
P.O. Box 363
Hulls Cove, ME 04644
Online: www.rebelsatori.com

10 9 8 7 6 5 4 3 2 1

Library of Congress Cataloging-in-Publication Data

Warren, J., 1974-
  Stealing Ganymede : a novel / by J. Warren.
     p. cm.
  ISBN 978-0-9790838-6-0 (pbk.)
  1. Assassins--Fiction. 2. Sexually abused boys--Fiction. I. Title.
  PS3623.A8646S74 2008
  813'.6--dc22

                        2008045127

for The Boys (Brian, Chrissy, Lucas, Brandon, Nathan, Jacob, Ben and Michael)

"...To Tros were born three sons, Ilos, Assarakos, and Ganymedes . . . Ganymedes, who excelled all men in beauty, was snatched up by the gods to serve as the cupbearer of Zeus..."

—Diodorus Siculus, *Library of History* (trans. C. H. Oldfather)

"...There is some pleasure in loving a youth, since once in fact even the son of Kronos, king of the immortals, fell in love with Ganymedes, seized him, carried him off to Olympos, and made him divine, keeping the lovely bloom of boyhood..."

—Theognis, "Fragment 1" (trans. Douglas Gerber)

1 • Epilogue

EVERY TIME YOU watch a movie about a man in my profession, it's always about the last hit he did. How he retired to Boca Raton. Or how the last hit went wrong and he ended up dead. One of the ones I saw had this guy from one of those cable shows, who usually plays a mob boss, as one of us. "Kevlar is for pussies" he says. I laughed hard. He wound up shot by a Hollywood pretty boy.

This isn't one of those stories.

This one doesn't move in a straight line. It can't.

I like the movies, though; the ones about guys doing what I do. It makes me feel—not understood, but—appreciated, I guess. I like the one about the guy who does hits to pay for his girlfriend AND his gold digging wife. He gets ulcers. Drinks Milk of Magnesia like water. That one was closer to the truth. I'm not telling you about my last hit, because it didn't happen. No. This is the story about the one that decided my whole life.

Not the first one, that one's easy. Like fucking for the first time; you sort of monkey your way through it and then feel like a man after. It's not until five, six years down the road you find out you botched the whole thing. That all your buddies were laughing at you behind your back.

They don't laugh anymore, though. Not after what you did to that guy in Louisiana. Most guys don't even shake your hand after that one.

I guess the question it all comes down to is, how do you become invisible? You can force it on someone. I know that much; but can you make it happen to yourself? The Professor would have said that being seen is just a habit no one knows how to kick. I tend to agree.

Skin and bone simply disappear and no one pays any attention. It happens about a thousand times a day all over the world. If someone isn't in the spotlight, they go quicker, easier. This was the last thing that Emmaus told me, then he disappeared. That's why I'm sitting here on this couch. In this hotel. In front of this coffee table. Looking at this gun.

This isn't one of those stories where the guy in my line of work turns into a blubbering simpleton after, or says some memorable lines and then you walk away feeling good. I'm not being played by any names on the hot 100 list of any magazine. No. I'm about as plug ugly as they come. In this line of work, it's not just a prerequisite. It's a skill.

But I'm not going to start into that now, though. I want to go to breakfast, but Gan is still asleep. It's so rare that I ever get to that point that I can't disturb someone who's there. Call it a failing of mine. I stub out the cigar and then go to the sink. Hot water. Gel. Razor. Mirror is already fogging up. Wipe it with my hand. Start cutting.

It was Emmaus who taught me how to shave. Taught me everything, really. Had to. I was on the street by fourteen. No sob story, just setting the whole thing. Way I see it, parents don't make any special contract with their kids. One day the kid isn't there, the next day he is. So what. So, one day I was there, the next day not.

I used to have to get real drunk to do the things I did to make money. You wouldn't believe how many sick fucks out there want nothing more than to get their hands on a kid as young as I was. If they can afford it, guys have been known to fly to Thailand, where that kind of thing isn't discouraged. They plan whole vacations to Prague. Maybe you would believe it, though. It wasn't all that shocking to me that kids did that sort of thing. No one had to tell me to do it. I just sort of knew.

Then Emmaus pulls up. Cadillac. Prada suit. Takes me to a hotel. Makes me keep the barrel of a gun in my mouth while he does his thing. After, he talked to me, though. That was the difference. Says to me, "Kid, you got the Knack." I could hear the capital K. Asks me, "If you could do anything in the world, no limit, what would it be?" and I told him. "I want to be a Rock star." I was fourteen, what the hell did I know?

He laughed that eerie laugh of his. Then he told me what he did for a living. I was in awe for about ten minutes as he spoke, then I realized that was it. That's what I wanted to be. And I told him. And he said, "Are you sure?" and I said yeah. He asked me again, said, "Don't fuck around, kid. You can't go back once you're in." What the hell did I have to lose?

He taught me what I needed to know about the business. And sure, he wanted action from me whenever he came back in, but he was teaching me. Every gig comes with its rules for incoming talent. You should see what they do to new porn stars. But, I'm pretty sure that, if there was a union for guys who do what I do (and I'm not saying that there is, but if there was), it would be against the rules. Not that that would stop anyone.

It was kind of an unwritten rule, he said. How else was I gonna pay him back? When you give your word, you give your word. So, you bury your face in a pillow and you grind your teeth together and take it like a man.

So, here I am. The American Dream. Now *I* have a Jaguar. Now I'm putting on my Prada jacket. Slide Virginia into her holster. Then Wolf.

The elevator ride down to the lobby is quiet. Muzak version of 'Sympathy for the Devil'. I laugh. I remember when that song used to be deemed as unplayable. Ultimately taboo. Now it was on the speakers in an elevator. All the piss and vinegar drained out of it. Mick would scream. Old Mick would, anyway. I doubt anyone has any real idea what hearing this vanilla'ed up version of this song means. To me. To most of us out here just getting by, now, in a world that had no piss left in it, with no promises left. Didn't want the devil as a lifeguard or as a best friend.

I'm on my way to go find him. I'll know him when I see him. I wonder if he'll know me.

The doors ding politely, then open. It was something straight out of a movie: The curtain opens, new scene.

2 • Dubois Is Late

ANOTHER CITY. Years ago.

"Did you sleep okay?" Gan asks. He's still asking. Three days and he's still asking.

"No," I answer. He keeps looking at me as if expecting more. There isn't any more, though. He asked, I answered.

He looks away out the window. The sunlight comes in and slides over his face. I'm telling you, I'm no fucking pansy ass painter or poet guy, but if I was, this is what I'd paint. Muscle, bone, sinew, skin. It all glows when you're that young. I'm envious of it. Because being an ugly killer is an archetype: being a beautiful killer is something that lands you in the picture books. They call beautiful killers Assassins, not hit men. I'm sure the Union wouldn't like that. If there was one.

"You don't ever talk."

"You do enough for both of us."

He looks back at my face suddenly, as if stung. I do my best imitation of a smile. His eyes lower a bit with his chin, and his return smile spreads slowly, like warmth across skin. Again, if I were a sculptor, this would be what was hidden in the stone.

He waits for what he thinks is long enough, then "Why are we here?"

"To get breakfast."

"I know *that*, I mean here. This town."

"This is a city. Towns are smaller."

I let it end at that. He wasn't satisfied, though. Of course.

"Okay, then. Why are we in this *city*?" he asks.

"Because—" I start to say, but the waitress shows up. Becky, her little silver nametag says. It's crooked. I notice this, along with the fact that her tennis shoes, though old and worried with lines of use, are immaculately white. She was in a hurry this morning, then. Women who take that kind of care of their shoes don't let their nametags hang crooked.

"Hi!" she says, "I'm Becky. I'll be your waitress this morning. Start you gents off with some coffee? Juice for your son?"

I knew it was coming. Gan just looks at me. "Becky," I say, tasting the name on my tongue. Her face draws back for a half a second. Her eyes dilate a fraction. I put more warmth into my voice, "I'll have coffee, and he'll have eggs. Two. Scrambled. Toast. Strawberry jelly." The image comes to mind of a snake toying with a rat just before it eats. Becky walks away much slower than she first arrived.

Leaning in close, "She thinks I'm your son."

"And there's no reason to draw attention by correcting her, is there?"

"Huh?"

"Later today, when her boyfriend, or girlfriend, or whatever asks 'how was your day?' I want her to be able to say 'boring.' I don't want her to have any stories about this odd man who came in and insisted that the boy he was traveling with wasn't his son. I don't want her curious, and neither do you." n-eye-ther. I'd been doing that since I was a kid. Leftovers from school.

"Oh!" he said. Bright. Just maybe bright enough.

She comes back with a mug. Pours in the coffee and dumps three little plastic containers of creamer onto the table. They are ice cold. Little beads of water collect on them.

"I forgot to ask if you wanted anything, hun," she says as she pours.

"Orange juice," Gan says.

She smiles, congratulating herself on a boy who wants his vitamin C. Then walks away. Very American.

"So, why?" Gan asks

"Why what?" I ask back.

"Why are we here in this town, I mean, *city*," he corrects himself.

"Because Dubois is late."

He waits, again, as if I'm going to say more. When it becomes apparent that I'm not, "Who's Dubois."

"Someone who's not going to be very happy about me showing up on his doorstep."

I can see the question start to form on his face before he even knows it's coming.

"Can I come?"

"No."

"Why?"

5

Just then Becky shows up with his orange juice and sets it down in front of his left hand, with a "Breakfast will be right up, boys" and walks away.

"Why?" he whispers, leaning in toward me.

I could take him. Sure. If things go sour with Dubois (and I am banking that they will—after all, if you have the money to pay Mason on time, you pay Mason on time. End of discussion. Most guys don't dick around with late fees in this business. Dubois knows that), what's the kid gonna do? Go to the cops? But, I'm hoping that it don't go so far south I gotta shoot the man. And if I come in with a kid on my heels, Dubois is gonna play that card. I know he will. I would, why shouldn't he? But, how do you explain that to a kid?

"Zeus—"

"Shut the fuck up. Right now. No. End of story."

And, something in my voice must've told him that it was. Because it was.

3 • Late Fees & Samurai Masks

LET ME GO back a bit, though. Show you how the end of all of this started.

Back then, Dubois lived in Uphill Estates or something like that. Rich places always have posh names. The apartments always have gold numbers on the doors. The other thing they all share is a lobby guy. Some call him the Doorman, some call him the Bellhop—some just call him security. Mostly, this guy is part time. He sits in the lobby with his feet up on the desk, drinking his hot coffee and farting. He might read, if he can read. Or he might play solitaire, laughing a little to himself if he wins a hand.

When you walk into a building on a job, it's like punching in a time clock. You put your game face on, like all those armchair quarterbacks say. Outside the door to the poolhall, or restaurant or apartment house or wherever, you might be laughing or joking with another guy who dropped a box. You might help him pick that box up. But, when the door opens and you step through, the curtain goes up.

Being ugly is a talent in this business, but having a good game face is even better. Samurai used to wear these terrible masks so that they looked like demons coming straight out of the center of the earth to devour their enemies. A buddy of mine told me that once. He had been good. Until he'd forgotten to pay Mason. It was a shit job, but I got the call on that one. As he croaked, he told me that I had the talent.

I told him "thank you."

As I pass into the lobby, the door swishes closed behind me. The security guy looks up. He's old. In his hand? Half a deck of cards. He takes his feet off the desk and puts them on the ground, sitting up.

"Can—can I help you?" he asked. A few of the cards slipped out of his hand. An ace of hearts and an eight of diamonds.

I don't even look down. This is the fun part. "Dead man's hand," I say.

He looks down quickly, then back up.

"Dubois," I say.

The man pushes the chair back on its wheels a little, "I'm afraid he's not—"

And that's when it happened. Just like in a damned movie. The elevator door opened, and Dubois stepped out. Tall, lanky. Sweaty guy. You could imagine he was the type of kid who always used to weasel his way along with his older brother and friends by threatening to tell mom about the playboys under the bed.

He saw me, but didn't register who I was for a second. He'd seen me enough times before, that was for sure. I was always at the poker game. Mason liked having one of "his boys" around as a bit of added insurance that things didn't go hinky. You could see it hit him, though. He stopped, looked like a deer in headlights. His eyes darted from the security guy back to me.

"Uh...hi," Dubois said.

I tipped my head slightly.

"Mr. Dubois, this gentleman was just coming in to see you," the old man said. You could hear the relief in his voice. His job was done.

"Ah. Was he? Good. Umm, Zeus? Is that it?" he asked, backing up a little as I strode toward him.

I didn't answer.

"I was just coming to see Mr—" he started, then thought better of it. His eyes darted again to the old man. Then back to me. Then back over his shoulder. I was herding him back onto the elevator. He licked his lips and swallowed.

I really liked this part.

The elevator doors slid closed behind us. There. Offstage. Time to let my hair down.

"I was just coming to see Mr. Mason—" he started.

"Save it," I said, standing with my back to the doors. He was a tall guy, I had to give him that. He only came up to my chest, though. His eyes slid under the jacket. He could see Virginia clearly from there. Good. He knew what this was about.

"Look, I can get—" he started, again.

I brought my flat palm up squarely into his face. He bounced off the rear wall of the elevator, and back into me. His face smacked against my chest. I could tell his front teeth had just hit Virginia's handle. That can't have felt good.

"OW! FUCK! YOU DIDN'T HAVE TO—" he started.

I brought my hand up and he cowered away from it. I brought my finger to my lips with a "shh."

"No bullshit here. Do you have forty-seven grand, in cash, on you, or in your room?" I asked.

He hesitated for a second, "I can get—"

Again, my palm, his face. Blood this time, although he kept himself from bouncing forward. He learned very fast.

"Do you have forty-seven grand, in cash, on you, or in your room?" I asked again.

You could see him thinking. He knew what happened if he said no. But he couldn't say yes, because he didn't. And he didn't think I was going to let him explain.

"I have twelve of it in the bank. I can get that out as a down payment if Mr. Mason—"

The elevator dinged. He hadn't seen me press the button for his floor. He looked over my shoulder at the panel. I hit him again. More blood.

"Never look away from your enemy. It's a sign of weakness." I think I read that somewhere. One of the books the Professor gave me.

"If you'll just let me get the money and take me to Mr. Mason, I can-"

I grabbed him by the arm and moved with him out into the hallway. I put on my smile. No one was in the hall, though, so it dropped. I moved him down to his door.

"Open it."

He reached in for his keys. He fumbled the key home and managed to undo the deadbolt. The door swung open and I shoved him in hard. I closed the door. He watched, fascinated, as I locked it. I turned to him.

"Do you know what it is I do, Lincoln?"

His eyes got big. He didn't know I knew his name. It seemed so much more personal, now.

"You're a hit—hitman?" he said, getting his mouth around the words.

"Something like that, yeah. It's not right, but I'm not going to bother to correct you. I solve problems, Lincoln. And you've become one." I'll admit, I love this corny bullshit.

I started moving toward him. He backed away from me, only looking over his shoulder when his ass hit the back of the couch and he nearly toppled. I took my jacket off and set it on the back of one of his white, wooden dining room chairs. He could see Virginia and Wolf fully, now.

9

You could see him get the full weight of how serious it had become.

"Oh, shit. Oh, shit. Look, there's no need for—" he started.

I raised my finger to my lips, again.

"Pick up the phone," I said.

He looked around frantic for a moment, trying to remember where he'd put his phone down. Finding it, he almost seemed to leap at it. He had it in his hands. They were trembling.

"Dial the office."

"What office."

My head tilted a little toward my left shoulder.

"Oh. Oh. Ohkay." He dialed the eleven digits very quickly. You could see him take time with each one, though, to make sure he punched it correctly. Then he brought the phone to his ear and stared at me, eyes glassy.

"No. Put it on speakerphone."

He stood there, not seeming to register that for a moment. Then he walked over and punched the button, setting the receiver down.

"Lutton and Associates." The bright female voice came out over the phone.

"Hi, Jenny, it's Lincoln—" he started.

"Jenny. Zeus. Put him on," I interrupted.

He leaned his weight against the back of the couch. His shoulders slumped, his breathing erratic.

"One moment, please," Jenny said.

Then there was muzak. It was 'Eleanor Rigby' by the Beatles. I couldn't help but laugh. It seemed like a theme for today. I wondered for a second if the kid even knew who the Beatles were.

It was interrupted by a thick southern accent, "Yeah?"

"I got him here," was all I said.

Dubois turned his whole attention to the phone as though Mason were there in the flesh. It was fascinating to watch. I got the image in my head of a praying mantis towering over a cricket, its head turning from side to side.

"Outstanding. Lincoln Dubois. How nice to hear from you, son. Hell, I'd just about given up on hearing from you at all."

"Mr. Mason, I can explain—"

"No. No, I'm afraid you really can't. See, two weeks late—that's an 'I can explain.' Three weeks is pushing it. When a man owes you Sixty-five grand..."

"What?!," Dubois interrupted, unable to stop himself. Immediately, his head jerked in my direction. He knew what was coming.

I didn't disappoint him. The blood sprayed all across the carpet and there was a wet, loud 'crack!'. It took him a second, but he did get up off the floor. I had to give him that much.

"Zeus?"

"Yes."

"If that boy interrupts me one more time—" He let the threat hang there a moment. I said nothing.

"But, Mr. Mason, I thought that it was forty-seven—" he started.

"And right you were, my boy. Forty-seven it was—when you skipped town three days ago. Now it's sixty-five. I had to send my biggest, meanest dog after you, and he ain't free, boy. After all, the man's gotta put food on his table somehow, right? Plus, you skipped town. That incurs a charge all its own. So, add it all up, and it comes out to a nice round figure like sixty-five. Call it late charges," Mason said. I could hear the smile in his voice, "Question is: do you have it? And I think I know the *answer* to that question, don't I just?" there was silence.

To his credit, Dubois waited. But not long enough. "I don't have it."

"See, now that is very, very bad news, boy. Do you know what that means?" Mason said.

The resignation was there in the slumped shoulders, the dropped eyes. He could see there was no way out of this. Funny enough, though, he didn't know what I knew. This was the good part.

"That you're going to kill me."

There was the sound of raspy laughter on the other end of the phone. After a count of three, Dubois head rose and he peered sideways at the phone. His eyebrows knit together.

"Well, I suppose I could just have Zeusy over there turn your head into a canoe. I could do just that, couldn't I, boy?" Mason said, still laughing, his voice all crackles and pops over the speaker. He knew I hated it when he called me that. I watched Dubois the whole time. His face registered some hope. I almost felt sorry for the guy. My hand went into my pocket and found the syringe there. I pulled it out.

"But, then I wouldn't get any of my money. And Zeusy over there would get all the satisfaction. Wouldn't he, though. No. I still have to find a way to get sixty-five grand outta you, boy. And I have just the thing."

Right on cue, I was just to the right of Dubois and the syringe went into his neck. The plunger was down before he even really knew what had happened. Too late. I stepped back.

"See, there's men out there who are lonely, Lincoln. Very lonely—and very wealthy. And some—well, some just plain ain't right in the head, do you follow me, son?" Mason said, the laugh gone out of his voice, now. Dubois was rubbing his neck furiously and his face was going slack. He looked very confused.

"And so I provide a bit of a service for them. For a nominal fee, of course. Now most, most are just your run of the mill sickos. Little girls, little boys, you know the type. But some? Some want more exotic entertainment, you could say. And I help them out when I can. Call me a good Samaritan. Ain't I just, though?"

Dubois was hearing, still. You could tell. He was having trouble standing up, but he was hearing. He tried to look over at me, but it was so slow that I doubt he even made the complete turn before he felt dizzy and disoriented.

"And so, that's what you're going to do for me, Lincoln, my boy. You are going to make my sixty-five grand by helping me out with a little request I just got about a week ago. Truthfully, I feel indebted to you for it. This man is a good close personal friend of mine. I didn't know that I was going to be able to help him out with this one, but it looks like I'm gonna be able to, thanks to you. Much obliged," Mason said. Somehow, he had timed it just right, and Dubois slumped into my arms at that precise moment.

"He out?" Mason asked, hearing the soft thump.

"He's out," I said.

4 • Goodbye Jimmy Marshall

THAT'S HOW THINGS went the first time I met Lincoln Dubois. That led to me hauling him down across the border to the Hacienda of a guy we'll just call Ted. You know him. In fact, you don't touch a thing in America that one of his companies doesn't manufacture some part of. I kept Dubois drugged the entire time. That's pretty much standard for something like this. But, it was when I got there that things went off script.

It had been hot as hell that day. That's a really common thing to say, and I'm sure people in hell don't think it's all that clever, but I don't mind. It was incredible, even to me, how hot it was. I was sweating pretty badly when I pulled the Suburban into the dirt driveway. I had read in a magazine once that the place was valued at about half a mil. I've seen that much money before, I won't lie on that account. It wasn't mine, but I saw it.

It was a big stack.

So I shut the Suburban off and waited. Right on schedule, a short, brown man came out of the door. He sauntered over to my side. Slow walk. Obviously not one of the hired help. Just under his jacket, I could see it: .9mm. I doubted it was the only one he had.

I rolled down the window.

"Can I help you, seen-yore?" he asked. Fake accent. More than likely Texas pretending to be Mexico.

"Delivery for your boss. Mr. Mason sends his regards." The man snapped his eyes, which had been wandering toward the rear seat, back to me. His lips thinned a little and he nodded. Then he turned and hurried back inside.

"Mmmf," Dubois said, shifting his weight a little. The dose was probably wearing off. He'd be awake soon. That was bad for him.

That's when it happened.

The door opened again after about three minutes. Out came a woman. She was trim, but not too skinny. Her calves were toned, her hair perfect. She was carrying a pistol, too. When she got close enough, her eyes were emeralds set deep in her head.

"Mr. Dallas?" She asked.

"Yeah?" Of course it wasn't me. She didn't know that. Most of the world didn't know that.

"He's expecting you. If you could pull the truck up over to the side and bring the package in, please?" She said, motioning in that direction. I couldn't take my eyes off her hands. Thin, long fingers, perfectly straight. Mine on the steering wheel were thick, hairy.

I pulled the truck around and got out. She stood watching from the driveway with Mr. Argentina next to her. His eyes were sweeping the road, his hand on his gun. Good boy, if a bit overzealous. She still stood there, though. Graceful and dangerous. I dunno. I'm not good with that wordplay shit.

I got out and opened the door to the back seat. Dubois was lying there, drooling on the leather. It figured. Tall as he was, he was still light. I pulled him out and draped him over my shoulders. Like that lion thing that Hercules wore in the story. I closed the door and walked over to the house. Some short old woman opened the house door for me and I walked in.

Nice houses always smell good. I noticed right off that this place smelled of that wood that they make chests and stuff out of. And food. I was hungry. As I carried Dubois around to the stairs going down to the 'playroom' (no, Dubois was not the first guy I'd ever delivered here), I also noticed that feeling. I was being watched.

I didn't bother with it, though. This was one of those kind of jobs where you get in and get out as fast as you can. All kinds of things can go wrong if you start fucking around with a man's play toy. Down the steps, it got colder. The walls stopped being painted. Long hallway with no lights to a thick metal door. It opened before I got there. I never saw the guy who held it open. More stairs, this time metal. Hollow thunk from each one as I went down them. Temperature drop. Hum of machinery.

"Mmf," Dubois said, shifting against my shoulder. Hands twitching. He wouldn't be out much longer.

Finally, no more steps. Large room filled with all kinds of odd shaped tarps. The smell of sweat and disinfectant cleanser. And something else. I smell it all the time, but there's no word for it. It's that smell around guys who like death. Not to die, but death itself.

"Dallas?" I heard him before I saw him.

"Yeah," I say, stopping. Waiting. Guys like this, they always want to make an entrance. Don't ask me, man. I don't know.

"Ahh, good. And this must be—?" Still, no show.

"Marshall. Jimmy Marshall," I say. The less this guy knows, after all, you know what I mean?

From around the side where there must be a hall or something, he comes in. He's got on a suit that, by the cut of it, probably cost him more than I'll make on this job. That's a lot. Pale and gaunt, I guess, are the words. Your typical bad guy type, really. They do all start to look the same after awhile.

"Mr. Marshall. Excellent. Well, if you could just put him over here-" he says, turning his back to me. Something inside me wants to pop him one for doing it. It feels like something old. I follow him, instead.

Around the corner, he's got this bed rigged up. Straps, cuffs, etc. It's segmented, so that he can use whatever length of it you need to. The ultimate in Modular Furniture. If you happen to be a pervert. He's gesturing in that direction, so I set Dubois, now 'Jimmy Marshall', down.

Off to the side, Ted has three guys. Not a one of them under two fifty of solid muscle. All dressed in leather. Kink stuff, you know? Codpieces bulging. Ted can hardly contain his joy. He's dancing around. He throws back the tarp covering a table nearby like one of those black and white movie mad scientists. Under that tarp are fifty of the most gruesome tools I've ever seen. Surgeons would shudder and, likely, wet themselves at seeing this stuff. Vintage WWII, I can imagine.

As if reading my mind, "These are authenticated to be Mengele's personal tools. I bought them at an auction in—" he says, almost spilling the beans in his excitement, but visibly stopping himself. He brings up a finger to his lips as if shushing the part of him that wanted to tell. That wanted that entrance. "Well, an auction, anyway. Would you like to stay, Mr. Dallas? I'm sure this will be quite entertaining," he asks.

Already the men have come forward and are stripping Dubois/Marshall down to nothing. The clothes are going, piece by piece, into a garbage sack. The guys are each wearing thick green rubber gloves.

"No. I have to get back. Mr. Mason said that you had—" I start.

"Oh, yes yes. He's upstairs. Drinking milk and cookies, I suppose," Ted says, giggling a bit, like a little girl. He's already turning his attention to naked Dubois being strapped in. As I turn around for the stairs, I can see that Dubois is waking up, his eyes slowly starting to open.

I almost feel bad for the guy.

5 • Falling

U P THE STAIRS. I was almost afraid I wouldn't make it before the
screams started. Back down the hallway, and up more stairs. I
was back in the house, which looked almost sane, just as a clock
somewhere struck noon. Big chimes. Goosebumps.

I walked back toward the smell. Tortillas and some kind of cheese. It was
good. I was really hungry. Someone humming in that direction. I won't talk
about the halls or go into all the rooms I passed. Just picture modern day
splendor at its best. *Better Homes and Gardens* cover story. That kind of shit.

I entered the kitchen, half hoping that the humming was the woman
from before. It wasn't. Sitting at a very long counter was a boy, his back to
me. At first, with his shape and movements, I thought he was a girl. I can be
honest about that part.

As if hearing me, he turned. He was Chinese or Japanese. I've never been
good at telling them apart, although they seem to have no problem with it.
Shiny black hair, brown eyes. Although, he seemed almost to glow. I dunno.
Like I said before, I'm not a poet. Jeans, T-shirt with something written on
the front. He was eating a chocolate chip cookie. In front of him was a large
glass of milk. He stopped chewing for a second. His humming died away.

I stood there. Quiet. His eyes traveled up and down me, then met mine.
There was a question in them. I answered it.

"Are you taking anything with you?" I asked.

His head moved from side to side. I stood there. Quiet. He got up off the
barstool and set the cookie down.

"Good. Drink your milk and let's go."

He tipped his head back and poured the whole glass of milk into his
mouth. A little spilled down the side of his cheek. I looked away. He wiped
it with his hand and set the glass down. I turned and went back the way I'd
come. I could hear his sneakers behind me.

"I'm Gan," he said.

I wanted to maintain my tough guy routine, but "You can call me Dallas."

"Is that your name?" he asked.

"I didn't say if it was or not. I said you could call me that."

"Oh," was all he said. He had to walk very fast to keep up. His legs were a lot shorter than mine. I've never been very good at judging ages on people. But he was about five foot, maybe five one. From the sounds he was making, maybe a hundred pounds, if that.

The Suburban was already up to fifty on the main highway before either of us spoke again.

"What's this guy Mason like?" he asked.

I don't get asked that question very often. Images of a dog baring its teeth and snapping furiously at something, held back by a chain around its neck.

"He's not the kind of guy you want to fuck with," I said. It was my stock answer. I really didn't know any other.

He started laughing. Kind of a desperate, thin laugh, though.

"What's funny?" I asked. Old paranoia. Old scars. I don't want to go into that.

"Nothing," he said, his smile already cooling to a grin.

"No, tell me."

"It's nothing."

"Fucking tell me," I said.

"You sound like one of those cheesy movies," he said

I didn't say anything.

There was a pause, "I was just thinking that he probably won't be 'the kind of man I want to fuck with'" he said, doing an imitation of my voice, "but it's not like I have much choice."

I didn't get it.

Getting through Border Patrol is pretty easy if you know some tricks. I do. Laugh a lot, tell a joke, let them search anything they want to. Never let them see you get nervous, right? Like those deodorant commercials.

It happens just after we get across.

The unthinkable.

He starts humming along with the radio, closing his eyes and leaning his head against the window. The light hits him just right, his hands tapping out a beat on his legs. He's in his own little universe. I catch myself watching him more than the road.

Something in the back of my skull is screaming at me to look away. To just drive the van. I'm thinking about how warm the window must be against his skin. I'm thinking about how it must be nice to just relax instead of worry about the next 'client'. I'm thinking about him in his own universe, completely oblivious to me. I'm thinking about how I want to be there. It's a moment, and you can't describe those moments with words. Words only get in the way when you try. Like it's a secret they don't want you to tell. Words are clumsy that way.

I fell for him.

I'm not stupid. I knew what the kid was for. Mason knew what the kid was for. Ted had already used the kid. It was how he made money. Lots of money. Most people are naive enough to think that it only happens in other countries, and only to women. If they only knew. And I did.

Most times, picking up and dropping off, as Mason said ("ain't that clever, though?") was easy. They were usually so strung out on Ecstasy or Cocaine that transporting them was just a matter of putting them in the backseat and driving. Like with Dubois. But this one? He's alive. He was singing to some stupid pop song on the radio.

I fell for him.

The job just became that much harder.

6 • 1072

INTERSTATE DRIVING ISN'T like life, no matter how many songs from the 70's say so. There's no metaphor there. The car almost drives itself. The wheel almost doesn't need you. They tell airplane pilots that: if you have to steer with more than a finger, you're doing something wrong.

Huge truck zooms past.

"Oxygen," the kid says, as he's playing with the radio.

"What?" I ask

"That tanker. He's carrying Oxygen," he says without looking up.

I wait, and when he says nothing, "How do you know that?"

"The D.O.T. number on the side," he says, looking up at me. His eyes catch the light and shimmer for a second. Like heat coming off of the road.

"What's a D.O.T. number?" I ask. I'm completely out of character for a moment. If this were a book, some English teacher somewhere would say 'your voice has shifted here; the character is talking different'. She'd be right.

"On all big trucks like that," he says, getting that look on his face. All kids get that when what they're thinking is 'idiot', "The Department of Transportation has a number they put on the side. So that if there's an accident, you can tell from a distance what's in the tank or trailer."

"And that one that passed us was..?" I ask

"Oxygen. 1072," he replies, going back to flipping stations.

"Where'd you learn that?" I ask.

"I know a lot of truckers. They like to show off," he said.

I wanted to ask more. I wanted to yell 'what did they do to you?', because I know what he means when he says he's 'known a lot of truckers'. Because I want to take each one of them and shoot them for what they've done.

Most of all, I want to know how this kid wound up doing what he does. Because there's always a story, and it's always a bad one. I've heard lots of them. Women, girls, men, boys. I've heard just about everything. Something tells me that when I hear his, though, I'm gonna bawl. I know it. It'll hit close to me.

"Nitrous Oxide," the kid says. Another huge truck pulls past us. The Suburban rattles a little as it goes by.

7 • Two Beds

NIGHT FALLS DIFFERENT on the road. Faster, somehow, less calm. You watch as huge roadside lamps sputter on and think about how far you've driven. It's a ritual.

I watch him open his eyes, and close them again, as we pull onto the off-ramp. Pretending to be asleep. Skill must've helped him out a lot. Most people wouldn't have noticed, it was so fast.

Town has a name printed in white up on the green board, but I've never heard of it. That makes it perfect. 'Food. Gas. Lodging' spelled out underneath. 'Yield' sign at the top of the hill, and I can already see the place. Huge brick rectangle with windows.

Pulling into a hotel for the night, he looks up. I see that look pass over him. This is familiar. And I hate that.

"Wait here," I say, getting out of the truck. He doesn't say anything, just stares out the window. His eyes are filmed over. He's somewhere else.

No one behind the counter in the cramped office. I stand at the desk for a second. We all do. Perhaps there are cameras. Some way for us to be seen without having to stoop so low as to ring a bell. I hate doing that. People remember you easier when you start demanding their time.

I stare back out the large, rectangular window. There he is. The streetlamps coming in from the windshield. The pose he's struck.

"I said, can I help you?" The woman asks.

Great. Already attitude. I turn to her. "Yeah. One room, two beds."

"Traveling with your son?" She asks. If she saw us pull up, then why didn't she come to the desk? Little power trips. That's America for you: little power trips.

"Sure. How much?" I ask.

She hasn't looked up from her computer screen, "$55.50, one night," she says.

I hand her a fifty and a ten. While she's working, I take a look around the place. Old habits die hard. Even a dog that's too old to hunt will still snuffle around for game when you let him out in the morning. Small desk behind the partition. Two cameras for the front of the building. Nearly 160 degrees of vision. Black and white, which means that during the daytime, people will get away with more, if they're fast enough about it: Unless it's dark, the picture isn't detailed enough to spot anything.

"Checkout time is noon. Ice machine's down near the pool. Enjoy your stay," she says, monotone. Her voice reminds me of instant coffee.

I get back in the truck.

"Two beds," I say.

He turns his head to me. Like an Owl would do. I can see that register in his head.

The room is small. You know the type. Cheap, bare, gray. Two sad looking beds. King James edition of the Bible in the drawer between them. One standard issue hotel room.

He walks over to the sink, looks at himself in the mirror. I can see his eyes get hard, brutal. He's being critical of himself. I can tell. I wonder which one of his parents he's imitating in his mind. He runs some water and splashes it on his face. Looks up and reaches his long, thin arm for a towel. Wiping his face off, he notices me watching. I'm sitting on the bed. He folds the towel and sets it to the side of the sink.

I want to ask. I am aching to ask. I don't ever get curious about things, but I'm on fire to talk to him. To find out what he dreams about. To find out how he came to this life. To find out why he's on his way to Mason. Although, I think I know that one. And it pisses me off.

"So—" he says, letting it hang there. He's turned toward me.

"So, what?" I say.

He walks over to me and stops. His hips are only as wide as my knees when they are pressed together. With one swift movement, he sits down on my legs, wrapping his legs around my waist. His lips are on mine.

Mine are on his.

"Stop," I say.

His head moves back from mine. I set him down on the bed. Move his legs from around my waist.

"What?" he says.

"Just stop. This is not like that," I say.

He leans away from me. He moves off of my lap in slow motion. His eyes get puffy, but never leave mine. His face turns red. He grabs the corner of the cover and wraps himself up in it. I turn and walk to the window. I can hear him trying to disguise the fact he's crying. That's worse to listen to than actual crying.

I don't know how to explain to him what I'm feeling.

How sex is the last thing I want from anyone.

Let alone him. And that's when it hits me. I know who he is in that instant. It's impossible. It makes no sense. But there it is. I guess I already knew it, but knowing and knowing are two different things.

So, no. I don't want sex from him.

Never him.

8 • The Abduction of Ganymede

THE CLOCK BESIDE the bed had cycled through nearly four hours. It was late. Or early, depending on your point of view. Einstein said that, I think.

Gan's head on my chest, his hand sliding along my belly. His thighs against mine, warm. I don't remember how he got that way. I felt something. Like...not hungry, only all over. Like the two of us close like that were really just one person lying on the bed.

"I love you," he said.

"Cut it out with that gay shit." I felt him recoil without moving.

"But—"

"This is something different."

"Oh," was all he said.

"You don't know me," I said before I could stop myself.

"I do, though."

"You just met me. I could be anyone. I could do anything."

"But you didn't," he said, pulling closer, "You're not a monster like them. I can tell."

"Shut up and go to sleep," I said, wondering how I'd gotten into this.

"I know you think you are, though—"

"Shut the fuck up. Now," I said, voice never changing pitch.

He lay his head back down on my chest and went to sleep there.

I couldn't sleep, though. When you transport merchandise, the main rule is that you never touch the merchandise. That goes for anything. Sports cars, cabbage, shoes, ships, sealing wax, you name it. The contract is you get paid to deliver the merchandise as it was given to you, no matter what that condition is. Only, he was sleeping on my chest. He had said that gay shit to me. And I almost didn't mind.

And there was no way that Mason was going to just let that slide.

9 • Mermaid

BACK IN THE car.

"I know this guy. One of Mason's best clients. He's got this huge underwater tank. Like you'd see at one of those huge places with whales and stuff. It's enormous. He fills it to the top with water. There are these two holes in the top, just big enough.."

"Just big enough for what?" he asks. Already with the questions.

"I'm getting there. Hang on. Anyways, just big enough. So he puts these girls in. Buys 'em, you see. Puts em in this tank and if they want air, they have to come up to these holes. Only, the hole is only just big enough for a nose and a mouth to fit in. So they have to tilt their heads up, like baby birds being fed. And that's when he does it," I say.

"Does what?"

"You don't want to know," I say, "only, now they have to take it, because they want air."

"Oh," he says, getting an image of what I might mean. I guarantee his image isn't nearly bad enough. But he gets real still, too. He's thinking about what happens when we get to Los Angeles. When the trip stops. And the work starts.

"'I always wanted a Mermaid' the guy used to say whenever I'd bring him a new one. Gave me the creeps."

"Oh," he says, turning his head to look out the window. His knee comes up to his chest, and he rests his elbow on his knee, propping his palm against his forehead. It's like a statue or something.

"Course, I don't know about no Mermaid. I'm just trying to get a paycheck," I say, smiling a little. I've made him sad. I want to undo that. His lips pull thin without looking at me.

"Hey, didn't you say that was Nitrogen?" I say, not really reading the number on the shiny tanker moving past us at light speed.

He doesn't look. I don't look, either. Eyes on the road. Straight ahead. One foot in front of the other was what Emmaus had always said.

"How did you get into this?" he asks. Tone lower. He's not looking.

"I could ask you the same question." Only, the way my voice sounds is "I kud axe yus the same qweshun". I guess.

He's quiet for a long time. Six more tankers pass by. I see him watching them go by. His eyes move slow, like he's not here.

"My mom died," he said. He was quiet for a long time, and I was about to say I was sorry, because that's the Christian thing to do, when he started up again, "She died when I was six. And dad, well, he kept saying 'it's so cold, Gan, it's so cold' so he'd come sleep in my bed," he said.

After another pause, he uncurled himself.

"It was okay for awhile. Shit, I even kinda liked it. You know, when you're that little, your daddy snuggling with you is okay. It was a year before his hands started to wander, so that first year was okay, I guess. And warm."

"What did your dad do for a living?" I asked, wondering out loud.

"He was a minister at this little church in Los Muertes. 'I tend my sheep' he always said, 'as you will, Gan. As you will'. He thought of himself as a shepherd. Me too, in a way. Or, at least, he wanted me to be."

"So how—" I started to ask quietly.

He jumped in, "So his hands started to wander—and not long after that, other parts of him, too. What the hell did I know? I was eight by the time it went far enough to hurt. And, I mean, he's my dad, right?"

There was a long pause, "I loved him. The church went under when I was ten. Dad never went back to his own bed. But when the church went under, he changed. He started to—to hurt me. I was scared."

I found my knuckles were white on the steering wheel.

"This guy dad knew was always looking at me. He scared me. He saw me one day at the market and asked me how I was. I told him I was worried. Papa was sick. Very sick, but I didn't have enough money to pay for the medicine the Doctor said he needed. That's all this guy was waiting for: An in. You can guess what happened. But it didn't end there. He knew we needed money with Papa not getting anymore from the church. And he had other boys."

I tried to relax my fingers, but I couldn't. They wouldn't loosen.

"But I was special. Mom was from Kyoto. She was Japanese. And I look it. So, he said, I could make more money than the other boys. 'My brown babies' he always called them, but I was always his 'rising sun'. So I did what he told me to do, went where he told me to go, met who he told me to meet.

Then Papa died, too. And I just didn't give a shit anymore," he said.

Another pause, "I made a lot of money then. I even got to keep some of it. For a little while."

I had to relax my fingers to get blood back into them.

I didn't say anything. I just turned my head to him.

"Sorry," he said, tilting his head to the side.

"So," I said, trying to get him to continue. It was like a car wreck. I didn't want to hear anymore, but I couldn't not hear anymore.

"What?" he asked.

"How did you—?"

"Oh. How did I get here?. The guy who was getting me places to live, and food, and finding me guys to go be with wound up owing some guy named Mason in Los Angeles. Mason wanted his money, but the guy didn't have it. So Mason saw me and said that I'd do. Said something about a customer who wanted a live in."

"A live in?"

"Yeah. He's buying me. For keeps. I'm his," he said, then tilted the can up, draining it in one long swallow. That last said in flat, lifeless tones.

This all happened before he said he loved me. This all happened before I told him that this is different, even though it isn't. Even though it isn't any different. This all happens before I want to tell him that I love him back. Even though it means I'm sick. Even though it means I'll hurt him. Even though he should be sitting in a classroom somewhere, wondering how to get in some girl's pants. Some boy's pants. It doesn't matter which. He should be there, worrying about whether or not his armpits stink too bad, or if his feet are too big. He should be worrying about how he's gonna get anyone to buy beer for him for July Fourth.

Only, he's not.

I'm taking him to Los Angeles, instead. And the cars passing by? They don't know that stuff like this really happens. They think about things like this and they think that book, the one the Russian guy wrote. They think an old, bald man on a park bench with a trench coat watching little girls on the swing. They don't think Fortune 500 guys in suits. They don't think twelve-year-old boys. They don't think about it because they can't handle that. They just want to eat their Cornflakes and move on.

Only, he's not.

I'm taking him to Los Angeles, instead.

10 · My Job

I CAN MORALIZE about my job if I want to. I mean, I grew up hard, but I'm not an idiot. How I think about God is this: you've got this guy with a garden, right? And he loves this garden, plants all kinds of things and gets off on watching them grow strong. But in every garden, weeds pop up, right? So, you've got this guy, and he loves this garden, and he's trying to keep it growing, only these weeds are everywhere. So he's constantly having to cut weeds away from the plants and flowers that he wants. Problem is that the weeds start taking more time than the plants. So what does he do? Well, smart guy that he is, he brings in something special. Something to eat the weeds and leaves the flowers he wants to keep.

Take a shark, for instance. People hate them; terrified of them. Good reason, too. On land, they're not much, but if you're stupid enough to tangle with one in his own territory?

Until things started to go screwy with the ozone layer and water temperatures went all wrong, you only found them in the real deep water. And should a guy be out that deep anyway? No. The shark keeps the ones smart enough out of water by just existing. It's scary, right? And the ones that are stupid enough to go out that deep? Well, those are weeds, and they aren't doing anybody any good. So they gotta come up.

Same concept, here. Usually, I don't have to do more than just show up someplace once, and for a month, everyone there is as cool as can be. Pay their bills up and everything. But every once in awhile, some idiot decides he's smarter than me. And he starts monkeying around with the natural order of things, thinking he's bigger than Mason. See, that means he thinks he's smarter than God. Those are the weeds. I'm here to eat them so God don't have to get his hands dirty. Like a guy said in one of those movies, 'if I show up on your doorstep, chances are you did something to bring me there'.

It was that way with Emmaus. He was beauty to watch; like a bolt of lightning. I seen him stomp in doors by himself. Double padlocks, too. Even when I wasn't short and skinny, anymore, he still towered over me, you know?

He was the hand of God. He taught me that. Pulling weeds. It makes me almost a priest.

And you always see guys in the movies sitting alone in a room, guns on the table, watching someone asleep on the bed. And they're smoking. And they're thinking about all the hits they've done. And they change. And I'm telling you it ain't like that.

It ain't like that at all.

Cause there's Gan, asleep on the bed, right now, and I'm thinking of finding out where this guy he told me about lives. Mason wouldn't like that. But Mason isn't going to like any of this. Is he gonna send one of his other bruisers after me? Likely, it won't be the kid. The kid isn't important in all of this. Chances are if he's got an order for a kid, any kid will do to the guy who's paying. And likely, Mason will have another boy to fill the order in about a day. A little inconvenience for a rich guy, a little sweat for Mason, but in the end? No big deal

It's the principle of the thing, though.

This kid is special. I can see that. Anyone could see that. And anyone watching this, if it was a movie (and it ain't, but if it was) would be judging me. But give them two hand-made .50's. Give them four twenty round clips. Give them a Kevlar vest that has one strap that won't go on right and always kind of hangs. Give them twenty-five thousand a hit, base price, without perks, and see what they'd do.

Give them Gan and see what they'd do.

Only they don't want to think about that. They want their Cornflakes, and they want their red and gray silk tie. They want kids to look cute in cough syrup ads. They don't want reality. They want some stupid sitcom where nothing bad ever happens. Most of them want that all the way up until I arrive on their doorstep. That's when they really start thinking about what they've been doing with their nights after work. It's always kinda funny in a not funny way. The power trip that comes on when they realize what's coming next. It's one of the perks of the job.

And I like my job. See, Mason isn't your average guy. He's got his hand in all kinds of stuff. A little of this, a little of that. Boxing, horses, poker, garbage disposal, prostitution and then this part. The Dubois part. The Gan part. How many people know that there has always been a black market for human beings? Slavery was ended, sure. But that stopped nothing. White, black, Indian (dots or feathers), it doesn't matter. You could say Mason is an equal opportunity employer, but that cliche has been in all the movies. Even if it's true.

And I'm his strong arm. He hired me for that. Emmaus was his boy before this. I remember being fifteen and meeting Mason. Big man in a suit. I was kinda in awe (you know how kids get) that such a big man could fit into a suit. I didn't know that suits could be tailored at the time, you know? I'd only ever seen them in Sears and on Emmaus, and he was a thin guy. What's the fancy word for that? Lithe. That's what made him such a great strong arm. No one ever saw it coming. Except that wolf grin of his. Again, being ugly is a skill.

"This the boy?" Mason asked as I came in that day. I went for a chair (I was young, what the hell did I know). I didn't realize there were only two in the room. And Mason was already in one. Emmaus grabbed my shoulder and did this twirling thing to me, where I spun out of his way and he never had to stop moving. One fluid motion into the chair. I wound up against the back wall. Mason kind of laughed.

"Yeah. That's him," Emmaus said, then. That raspy sound. Like a snakes belly.

"You already been at him?" Mason said. I had turned around at this point, and I could see Mason sitting up in his chair, his big belly poking a little over the top of the desk.

"What do you care?" Emmaus said, tossing an envelope onto the table. The guy we'd just gotten back from visiting.

Mason shrugged and counted it. Then nodded. Then we left. I didn't see him again for awhile. I never asked why. I learned everything I know from Emmaus. He was my real dad. Not that fuck in Wyoming. Not his bitch of a wife, either. I was born when I was fourteen, you could say, or you could tell the truth and say that I was born when I was twenty-five.

When I had to kill Emmaus.

11 • Like That Gatsby Guy

SEE, MASON IS always throwing these parties. Like that Gatsby guy. Huge gatherings of faces that you don't know, but you know. You've heard of every single one of these guys. Every day, you depend on something that they make. And there's not just boys at these parties, although there are a few of them. I know those faces. See them all the time around Mason's house. No. All kinds of entertainment is available at one of Mason's parties. Women, girls, men, those pretty, halfway-in-between people either very butch college age women, or very girly guys. All kinds of stuff. And mountains of drugs. You name it, you can find it. I bet the only thing Mason regrets is that he can't write the whole thing off as a business expense.

Maybe he can.

At any rate, Mason tells me to come to one. Off the clock. I was flattered, actually. He asked me if there were any special requests I had for him. I said "Yeah. Emmaus." And he frowned but said "Anything for a guest."

This is before Gan.

So I walk in the door. And mingle around with these people. This one guy, he owns a huge computer corporation. I bet you have one of his computers at work right now. This guy, he's got this woman on his lap, and he's got his hand up her shirt, pinching her nipple. And every time she makes a noise, he smacks her on the back of the head. You might think that's pretty bad, but to look at her face, this is heaven. She could be faking it, I'll grant you that. She could be that good. This is right as I walk in the door.

The music is some Latin guy doing warmed over disco. Whatever. I mean, who cares. Music is always in the background. I shoot people for a living, what do I care about who's 'number one with a bullet' on whatever chart. Who gives a shit?

"Take your jacket?" Some kid asks. He looks like he ought to be in a dorm room, somewhere, worrying about whether or not he's making too much noise when he spanks off in bed.

"Nah, kid. Thanks, though," I say, turning. As I do, I can see his eyes land on Virginia and Wolf. The guns are top notch, and big. His eyes go wide. He'd probably laugh to think a big guy like me actually reads.

But I do. It's funny: one of the first jobs I had to pull was this college professor. I won't go into why I was on his doorstep. Let's just say that he had made some pretty bad career choices on his last vacation to Mexico, and then forgot that gentlemen pay their debts. So, anyway, I have to do him at his house. After he got back, he didn't go out much. After I gun him, I start looking around. I do that sometimes. I'm only nineteen at the time. I would probably be in his class if I had gone along with what life is supposed to be. So I'm looking around and I find all these books that I've heard about. I mean, even if you don't read, you hear the names. So I start picking out the ones that have titles I like. One about sound and fury sounds cool. The one about the Gatsby guy, cause it calls him great right there in the title. Shit like that. And I do read. I mean, when you've got downtime, what else are you gonna do? Watch TV? That box makes you stupid and slow.

So the kids eyes hold steady on Wolf. He's too skinny to be a threat, so I turn my back on him and check out the rest of the party. That's when Mason shows up. He probably sent the kid over first. Like I said, you'd be surprised what lengths these kinds of guys will go to when they want an entrance.

"Zeus! How are you, boy?" Surprised that you can still move about under your own muscles, actually, I almost say, but don't.

"I'm cool," I say.

He takes my elbow in his hands and starts leading me further into the house. He's pointing out who this person or that person is. Only, we're going too fast, really. I don't catch half the names. Two more rooms down the line and there's a bunch of guys with violins and one of the other kind, the big tall ones that sit on the ground. I don't remember the names. Here, he introduces me to someone and my brain kicks into overdrive. Some blonde. Perfect sized tits, long, flowing hair. Mason leaves and she and I end up talking. Turns out she reads a lot, too. Ten minutes later, she and I are naked and making good use of a really thick mattress, upstairs. Like I said, this is before Gan. Things made a lot more sense then.

So, she's done and all exhausted. She can't really move and I ask her what I owe her. "Fuck you," she says, "I'm no whore." But it's all lazy. No energy. She's not even moving her head.

See, that's a shame. It means I have to hunt her down, later. Whores I can expect a certain amount of privacy from. Most of the good ones, anyway. This lady just wandering around knowing about my birthmark and what size of guy I am? No. Can't let that happen. I look back at her, one more time, to memorize her face. Got it.

It's as I'm coming out of that bedroom, all excited cause I have something to do tomorrow, that I run into him.

See, we hadn't seen each other in three years. When I turned twenty-two, I had already gotten two inches taller than him, and put on my death mask. He helped me to get my first guns (I didn't name them), and then, the next day, he just wasn't there anymore. And what was more important, is I kind of knew he wasn't going to be. We'd become so tuned into each other that I knew it was time. And even after not seeing him for three years, I knew him. He'd shaved off his beard, most of his hair and slimmed down, but it was still him.

I started to get all stiff again. It was okay, though. I came here to kill him.

"Marcus?" he asks. It's bullshit, though. He knows who I am.

My eyes never leave his. Not even when he uses the old name. The fourteen-year- old name. His eyes soften a bit around the edges. Mine don't. When they don't after a second, he knows. He sees. My hands fly for Virginia and Wolf.

Time moves all funny when you're drawing down. I wonder, sometimes, if it was like this for Samurai as they made that first pull of the sword in battle. There's this thing they used to do called Iajutsu. They would pull the blade and make one slicing cut at an opponent, and that cut would be so perfectly placed, and skillfully timed, that there wouldn't be any need for another. The guy would be dead and not even know it, it would happen so fast. The sword would come out, that same motion making the cut, then go back into the scabbard. One clean movement. Perfect. I wondered if time slowed down for them as they did it. If I ever find one, I'm going to ask.

But he doesn't start reaching for his gun until I'm already halfway to mine. Emmaus, he always carried only one gun. Said it was all anyone ever needed. Two guns was overkill, laughing at the pun. I didn't care, at that point, though. I knew he was going to leave me. I had seen it in his eyes.

And I saw it in his eyes right at that moment, too. He knew that he had hesitated a fraction of a second too long. Both guns were out and the slow motion flashes, like photographs, went off. Some sort of horrible photo, though, freezing the subject in his pose forever. His hand made it to the handle of his gun, I'll give him that.

Both my guns have silencers. Long, thin tubes with holes drilled in them to let the gas escape more efficiently, dulling the noise. And I know he's wearing one of those damned vests, so I aim one for the throat and one for the middle of the forehead, where the eyes meet the nose. Are those the best points to do someone? No. Lots better to get in close and use an eye socket. No real protection there. But, at this point, it's not about efficiency. It's about revenge. It's about completing the circle of life. Still, two guns, even silenced, going off at the same time in a hallway is not going to be totally quiet. I look over in time to see the bedroom door open, and the blonde walk out.

I do her one quick one in the eye socket without taking my eyes off Emmaus. That was about efficiency. Only it depresses me for a second. What is there to do tomorrow?

I'm looking down at Emmaus' corpse and thinking, 'Now, what?'

I'm walking out the back door onto the deck thinking, 'What am I going to do now that that's done?'

I'm standing near the edge of the pool, watching the way the light makes these curvy lines, all wriggling around on each other, like worms, and I'm thinking 'Emmaus is dead'.

And I'm remembering that first night, when he first put the gun barrel in my mouth. And the old me sort of slid aside. It dove deep down. And, maybe somewhere down there, I can kinda feel him moving around sometimes. Struggling to come up for air.

Just before I step over the side to drown myself, Mason is there at my elbow, again.

"Zeus? What are you doing out here, boy?" What is a guy as huge as you doing with a pool? I want to ask, in return. But I don't.

"Nothing," I say. "Emmaus is dead. Upstairs. Have Jeremiah go get him," I say.

And I leave.

And Emmaus is dead.

12 • The Swan

ACK IN THE place where we're having breakfast.
So we're sitting in this restaurant. And Gan isn't eating
anything, just sort of moving his food around. I can tell he
wants to talk, but he can see the mood I'm in today.

"So, who's Dubois?"

"An old friend." I don't tell him. Why should I? What do you tell the
kid? That the guy is miraculously back from the dead? That he's threatening
to rat on Mason if we don't pay him off?

That I've got to find a way to put a bullet in him before he can do that?

Gan is quiet again. The waffle moves around some more on the end of
his fork. He sighs.

"What?" I finally ask. I'm tired of the play.

"Nothing."

"Bullshit. What," I say.

"You don't tell me anything."

"Should I?" I ask.

His eyes get big around and his head moves backward on his spine
some.

"Yes," he mumbles, "no. I dunno."

I take another sip of coffee. Look out the window. Of course, I'm sitting
in the furthest booth from the door, with my back to the wall. That's just
instinct, these days. I don't even have to think about it. You sit with your
back to the wall, facing the front door with as clear a shot as you can get in
case someone comes in that you'd rather not see. Or, better, that you'd rather
not have see you first. Only one time, when I was real young did someone get
the drop on me like that. Everyone has it happen sooner or later, but it only
ever happens once. Either you die, or you live through it and never make the
mistake of sitting with your back to the door again. You can always kind of

tell who might be in the business by how they sit. And where.

And that is how I see Leeda come in the door before she sees me.

The tall girl from Mexico. The one at the house I brought Dubois to. She's got her jeans on, and her shirt that shows way too much of her belly button, trying to fit in. But Latino's never do. They have a natural sexiness that bleeds through. You always know when someone is actually from a Latin country. They can't blend it. And you never really want them to. It's like the language. It drips with sex.

She does, too

I watch her for a second, and I'm feeling more relaxed. I set the coffee down. She's got her jacket tied around her waist, and under it I can almost see her gun. She's good. Most people wouldn't think anything of the bulge on her hip. I see it plain as day, though. And I'm thinking about her thighs. And her mouth.

And that's when she turns and sees me. That's always amazed me: you can be looking right at someone until you actually are staring, and then they home right in on you. As if your sight was a laser beam for them to follow. It's kind of creepy if you see it happen too often.

So she starts coming this way. And I'm watching how she moves. How everything around her becomes graceful as she passes it. Then goes back to being ugly as she moves on.

And Gan sees me watching. And I can see that look in his eyes. He knows what I'm thinking. And he sees her. And his eyes close up some. His lips thin. His jaw sets.

"Hi," she says, stopping at the table, standing next to Gan's side. She's got her back to the door. Not smart. She's still new at this.

"Hi," I say. She's waiting for Gan to move over. He isn't moving.

"Gan. Move," I say.

He exhales and scoots his plate and himself over. He doesn't look up at her. Or at me.

She sort of breezes into the booth with us. I start looking at my hands. See how huge and ugly they were. I lean back and tuck them in my jacket pocket. I look at Gan. He's looking out the window. My eyes meet his in the glass. He was dark.

"So, has Mason—" When she says it, I freak out a little bit, yeah. I lean forward real quick and shake my head some. You never know when they've got your number. A salt shaker, a fork. Who knows what they've come up with to use as a microphone. Or worse.

"My boss has made me very familiar with the details," I say, clearing my throat. Gan drops his fork. He saw the sharpness in my eye, I bet. He and I talked about that before. But this is now.

She recovers herself, some. "Good. Then you've found him?"

"I wouldn't have had you meet me here if I hadn't."

"Good. Can you turn him over to us?"

"Oh, sure. Sure. Only, anything more than the name of where he's staying will cost you extra." There it was. She sat back some, her eyes wide. She thought that the name of her boss would cow me some. Screw that.

"Considering the nature of the mistake—" She starts.

I knew she would, "Look," I start, and her eyes dart over to Gan. She doesn't want him listening. I can tell. "It wasn't my mistake. I delivered him to you and took delivery of another package which, because you called me while I was on the road, hasn't been delivered yet. Now I got my boss breathin down my neck. Don't come in here telling me that I made a mistake and then expect me to believe you." I lean back again, stretching my arms out against the back of the booth's couch.

Her eyes tremble some. Her mouth thins out. She puts her hands on the table and folds her fingers over each other. She slides her eyes over to Gan again, then to me, quirking an eyebrow.

"Hold down the fort, kid. We gotta go talk," I say, standing up. She's sliding out, too. He doesn't look over.

I knew he wouldn't.

13 • Leeda and the Swan

I T'S NOT CONSIDERED out of the ordinary for the women's bathroom in most restaurants to be locked. She goes in, then signals me to follow. Inside, I'm more aware of just how big and ugly I am. This place is made for people who are used to nice stuff. Wallpaper. Mirrors. Stalls with doors. She locks the door behind us.

"You were promised six for finding him and returning him to—"

"No. I was promised six for finding him. I was promised three for delivery of him to you and whoever else you brought with you."

She waits. "I only have six."

"Then it looks like the name of his hotel is all you'll be getting," I say, and move toward the door.

And she grabs my arm.

See, don't get the wrong idea about me. Sure, I'm an animal, but this lady had some refinement. You don't just grab a guys arm, though. It's not until the gun is against her temple and the hammer half way back that I realize what's just happened. She's trembling, some, but nowhere near enough. I can tell this is not her first time. I ease the trigger back home. The hammer settles itself back into it's cradle. Everyone's all nice and calm.

Virginia goes back into her holster. And Leeda shivers, losing her balance. Exhaling loud. And moaning.

"You okay?" I ask, leaning down to grab her.

Which is when I noticed that her skin was hot, not cold. See, someone feinting, nine times out of ten, their skin is going to be cold from the shock of whatever. But her heart was hammering away and her skin was hot, and she was trembling. And then she said it. Those two words. Said out loud, you might be able to resist them. Whispered in your ear from a woman who's just had an orgasm because you pulled a gun on her—well—

I don't remember anything for about ten or fifteen minutes. Except telling her to be quiet. And wondering how we're going to clean up, after. And the squeaking of the cheap countertop not all the way glued down.

See, I hadn't done anyone the way Emmaus had done me. Not yet. No gun, you know? But she asked for it. I mean asked me to do it. To put the gun in her mouth. I dunno. I mean, what was I supposed to do?

Cleaning up in a sink is awkward at best. I knew we both reeked of it. And now my hair was all messed up. My huge hands trying to pat it down. My watch said we'd left Gan alone for twenty minutes. I couldn't help it. It wasn't going to be that long when the gun thing happened.

"Fine," I say. "Six and I'll go get him."

She stopped fixing her hair. Looked at my eyes in the mirror. Smiled some.

"Where are you staying?" I asked.

She pulled a matchbook out of her purse and handed it to me. Not too far. I walked out and over to the men's room. When I came out, she was gone.

Back at the table, Gan is asleep, his head resting on the glass. The light was hitting his nose and eyebrow just right. He looked so peaceful. I flopped a twenty and a five on the table, then reached into the booth and picked him up. I cradled him against my chest and carried him up the steps to the door. He mumbled once, and burrowed his head a little deeper into my chest. Then to the elevator. And up.

14 • Gan's Dream

*h*UGE MUD WALLS *on all sides and he's sitting against one of them cold penetrating through the thick wool that they said would help him it's not helping him not against the cold not against the rain and he's shivering his body just trying to do what it does to stay warm and it's not working at all to his left there is a guy who's head is down and he's praying in the vacuum of silence between shells night is a cold hungry wet thing pressing in all around the two seeming to tuck them in*

You think we're ever going to get out of this? *he asks there isn't any response he didn't really expect one somehow deep down he knows that the guy sitting next to him is really him that this war is being fought on some levels he doesn't even know what to call*

Hail Mary, full of grace, blessed of the—*the guy drones on not looking up his head burrowed down in his sweater jacket helmet as if a turtle*

there comes the beginning of a whistle a distant high pitched sound that could easily be mistaken for background noise the kind people call white noise only in his mind there is nothing white about this noise at all it means a shell incoming and the target might be miles off it might be right here though and that was what worried him but like the hand of God there is nothing he can do to stop it so he yells what you're supposed to yell

INCOMING! *he yells and hears the rustling of the fifty other guys in this particular trench who have suddenly appeared the whistle grows in slow strength soon it will be a deafening crack in the air around him and be unbearable and he knows that this time the shell is heading right for him that he is the actual target he and the mirror that is praying praying praying next to him while he waits for that he wonders if there will be pain and he gropes his brain for the name of the greek myth about the boy who loved his own reflection*

Narcissus *the boy next to him says who's stopped praying for a moment and goes right back to it*

Thank you *he says because that's what you're supposed to say and waits wondering if he's in love with himself and that's why the other version of him is sitting huddled next to his leg the noise grows grows horrible in it's growth like cancer or a boy who will one day become hitler or stalin or any american president horrible growing that can't be stopped unless there's blood*

and then he sees them.

just over the wall of mud out in the barbwire garden called no man's land by every poet in this trench pens furious writing in one hand cocks in the other furious working but out there in that barbwire there is movement and in that movement he can see monsters not the pretend ones in kids books but real ones faces shifting and moving on their own movie grins exposed crawling on bellies like snakes or men or spiders somehow not even touching the barbwire the razorwire with their own skin and he can tell they are all coming for him the grins are because they are coming for him and his reflection who is now singing and each time he repeats what he's singing he moves one of the tiny amber beads from his wrist to under his index finger

and then he sees her.

standing above them she's got a sword where did she get a sword from she's standing above them with a sword waving them on toward him and yelling her voice horrible amplified like a megaphone only she hasn't got one and the whole time that noise moving around and through him trying to destroy him from the inside to bake him like heat inside and threaten him with whispers of the pain to come and the language she's yelling in is that same language almost seeking him trying to pry inside him like fingers with no fingernails trying to get under a lid but the monsters seem to understand it and it makes them happy she is saying it singing it yelling it out

Gonna be one helluva show in a second *comes a voice from next to him and he thinks it might just be his reflection his (what? Narcissus. Thanks) other but when he turns he sees the other still praying the man who is next to him has the same extremely dirty uniform and is nearly as soaked in mud and blood and whatever but this guy is much taller and thicker he's a man full grown and he is*

(Zeus)

someone the boy knows and hears his name whispered only that isn't his real name he doesn't know what the man's real name is but it's not the name he's thinking of because that one implies thunder and the shell is getting closer because he can feel the heat already and the air is starting to leave in little evacuations of it's own

You gonna stick around for that, kid? *the man asks*

and the boy thinks maybe he might answer that only he can't he finds he has no mouth to speak out of but the man can't see that the man can't see anything other than the two enormous guns he has in his hands and the boy suddenly wants only to be held because if he has no mouth he can't tell the man how he feels how he truly feels and if only he had a mouth he would have a tongue and he might be kissed or loved or something other than frightened and about to die

and he thinks that maybe the man can do something about that

I'm not going to let you die *the man says*

and that's when he understands that the man knows what he's thinking and always has that the man sometimes lets him make his own mistakes but would never let him get really honestly hurt and he wonders for a second if this man might not be his father and as he thinks that the other (Narcissus. Thank you) self looks up with a blur of motion crisp around the edges but they both see that this isn't their father, this is some man with two enormous guns and a wolf-like grin on his face

and the man stands up and starts letting huge bolts of fire loose with those guns that sear the earth and incinerate the monsters as he does so and the boy can tell that this man is crying as he does this because the one monster he wants to slay is somewhere he can't reach those guns won't turn toward himself so it doesn't matter how many of them he destroys the one that needs destroying can't be it's immortal and the boy knows that there is only one thing that can destroy a creature that powerful a monster that huge a man that strong

it(him)self.

But the woman keeps commanding armies and she keeps advancing and he won't shoot her why won't he shoot her she's right out in the open the boy thinks that maybe he could take his gun and shoot the woman and he reaches down for his rifle covered in mud and he brings it up to his shoulder like they showed him and unlocks the chamber and yes there is a round in it and he closes the chamber again and he aims down the sight and that's when he realizes that the noises have all stopped no more grumbling crumble sounds of the monsters as they crawl toward him no more thunder as the man lets fly huge muzzled wolves to do his bidding no more groaning language no more shrieking shell only him and his heartbeat like in some bad movie and he's sighting down the barrel at her

and he realizes that if he kills her he kills the man too and somewhere inside he thinks that maybe that's best and he realizes that by killing the man he kills himself and leaves only the mirror self to pray and pray and pray like a good little boy he sees the golden wire that stretches from all of their hearts toward the other

and then offstage somewhere and the hush is over the crowd as he hears them saying his name over and over again
    gan—*Gan*—gan—Gan

15 • While You Were Away

GETTING IN FROM breakfast.

I put Gan down on the bed and the phone rang. No one's supposed to have this number. I propped Gan's head on the pillow and walked into the bathroom. Second ring. I turned on the faucet. Third ring. I pulled out the phone and slid the mouthpiece down.

"Where are you?" Mason's voice said almost before I could get the phone to my ear.

"You're the one who called," I say.

He laughs under his breath, then "Did the woman show up?"

"Yeah, you could say that."

"What do you mean?" Mason said.

"She showed up carrying. And asked for extra."

"Extra what?"

"Says her boss thought it was a carry out job."

"And?"

"She and I had a chat. I'm going to do it for her for a little extra."

"Fine. What about the package you picked up?" he asked.

I hadn't realized I'd paused until he asked, "Well?"

"It's alright," I answered.

"When can you get it to me. The gentleman is hungry and he wants dinner, heh." Mason laughed that dry laugh. Pervert.

"Who's it going to?" I asked.

"What the fuck do you care?" Mason asked, hardass all of a sudden.

"Because I want to know."

"Well, that's my business, then, isn't it. Isn't it just?" Mason said.

I paused again. This time on purpose.

"Margolise. You know the guy."

I got lost in flashbacks for a minute. Yeah, I knew the guy. I'd delivered a few to him before. Tall guy, nice suit. Eyes about the same shade as volcanic glass.

The first one I ever took to him had been shaking. I didn't pay any attention. Not my problem. The kid vomited some, too. I took him up to the room I'd been told to leave him. Hotel De Plaza, or something like that. One of those thousand-dollar a night places. I let him in, made him take a shower and threw his clothes down the garbage chute, like I was told to do. When the kid came out and asked where his clothes were, I dosed him with chloroform, like I'd been told to. He struggled a bit, then passed out. I put him down on the clear plastic sheet I had put over the bed, like I'd been told to, and walked out the door. I locked it, then phoned the number I'd been told to call.

"Is he up there?" The voice on the phone had asked.

"Yeah. Out cold. Door's locked."

"Good," he'd said, "At the counter, downstairs, turn the key back in and then pick up the envelope under your employer's name," he'd said and then the line went dead. I got a shiver down my spine. I was pretty young then.

I didn't find out until a year or so later what he'd done to that kid. Virgil and I had been talking when I'd taken some vacation time over in Spain. Virgil is the guy you call when you have something you want to get rid of, and it won't fit down the garbage chute. He said he'd never seen so much of a mess. I asked what he meant. Then he told me. And I puked. Not in front of him, though. You don't show weakness in front of anyone in the business.

Margolise had a habit of doing what he wanted with them, then going kind of off kilter. Cutting them up, after. What made it worse was that Margolise had been a surgeon before he retired. He was good at cutting. I bet the kid was alive for most of it.

I snapped back when Mason said, "What is it?"

My eyes went to the mirror. Then to the door. Then along the back wall of the bathroom to where Gan must be sleeping. Then they closed.

"Nothing. I'm going to be late, though."

"Not too late, now, boy. The package is expected by the end of the week." It was already Thursday.

My eyes snapped open.

"Okay," I said, and hung up.

Somewhere, about two thousand miles from here, Mason would be slamming the phone down. And cursing me. And lighting up a cigar. And cursing me some more.

I sat down on the bed and put my elbows on my knees. Leaning forward, I stared at the carpet. The guns were heavy against my chest. Margolise. Margolise had men of his own. Mason would get Virgil to come track me down. I knew that much. I could maybe pay Virgil off. The others, Margolise's guys, I dunno. I don't know them.

On the other bed, Gan was on his stomach, his head cocked to the side, his arm tucked behind his back. I leaned back on my elbows. I watched him sleep.

Fucking Margolise. See some of the guys, they just want the son they can't have. Sure, they wanted sex, too. That couldn't be helped. But they wouldn't hurt the kid. This was a different story, though.

Gan moved around some, mumbling. The guns were heavy against my chest. I took my jacket off and then sat still. The boy curled against himself. Like a baby in its mother's stomach. He made a noise like crying, only with his mouth closed. I watched.

I was actually tired. I hadn't slept. The boy must have stayed tired; the little bit of sleep he had gotten must not have been enough.

The guns hadn't really ever come off my shoulders before except to sleep. As I loosened them, first one and then the other strap, I started to feel naked. I set them down on top of the leather jacket. I walked to the bed and sat down. I put my hand around the boy's ankle and pulled his leg toward me slow. I pulled his shoe off. He flexed his foot a little. I dropped the shoe on the floor. I put the leg back where it was. I put my hand on the other ankle, pulled the leg toward me like the other. Pulled the shoe off. Dropped it on the floor, too. Put the leg back where it was. I toed out of my own shoes. He burrowed his head down further into the pillow. I stood up, moved around to the other side of the bed, then laid myself down next to him. He moved back against me, mumbling a little.

I put my arm around his waist. I was like that for a long time, waiting for sleep.

16 • Zeus' Dream

I<small>T DOESN'T MATTER</small> how fast you really are at it, pulling your guns always feels like trying to swim through motor oil. No. Thicker. More like Jell-O. And no matter how many times you do it, it's always going to feel like that. But in a dream, where everything feels like that already, it's even slower. I remember this one movie where the special effect was like that: perfect slow motion. You could even see the bullets and the little sonic waves they made because they traveled so fast. I thought 'that's exactly it'.

My dreams are always like that, too. I remember as a kid, before I'd ever even fired my first gun, I would dream my toy guns were real. That the guy I was standing in front of in the dream had real ones. I would always see him moving impossibly fast, and knowing. Knowing. That he was going to get them out and pointed before me. Somehow, though, in my dreams, before he could fire, the scene would shift.

And then we'd be fucking. Wild, crazy rubbing against each other, really. I mean, I was five. What does a five year old know about sex, other than it has to do with rubbing. I dunno. I'm not a psychologist. I bet it means something deep and complex.

In my dream, I'm wearing white feathers. And Leeda? She's got the guns. And I'm standing there defenseless. She shoots me. Grinning. I have my guns halfway up as she's already getting the next round into the chamber (she's using one of those cheap one-load-only carbine deals). Only, when I look down at myself? It's not me in the white feathers anymore. I'm in Gan's body. I'm Gan. Naked. And bleeding. And she's grinning. Then me, the real me, is behind her, fucking her senseless. And the Gan me is bleeding. Dying.

And I wake up.

17 • The Little Fisherman

S o, WHAT WAS it like for you as a kid?" Gan asks.
He's standing in front of me in the shower. He runs his hands over his face. I put soap on my hands and rub it on his shoulders.

"I dunno," I answer. *brief flash of cold air on my ass and then the sound of a slap from a million miles away.* Somehow knowing I was scared that slap meant I'd been hit, but not remembering if it hurt.

"You don't remember?" he asks. He stops for a second and turns his head a little over his shoulder to look at me sideways.

"No," I say. I turn him around so the water hits his back. He's looking at me.

"No?"

"I just said. No."

"Oh," he says and looks down.

I knew a guy, once, one of Mason's big money clients, kept a harem of boys. Never wanted to have sex with any of them. Just wanted to shower with them, eat with them, cuddle up with them. There were over thirty that I knew of. Here, it couldn't have happened. But where he was from, no one even batted an eyelash. "Where he's from, Z, they say women are the holiest of holy. For procreation only. Little boys are for recreation. Aren't they, though," Mason had said, chuckling.

I had to take a boy to him. A young one. I didn't care. I was just a kid myself, really.

Guy ended up dead, though. He never touched them, but that didn't stop them from touching each other. Couple of the older ones got all hung up over the new boy and decided they didn't want the old man touching him. They wound up lynching the guy. Kids can be pretty vicious if they put their minds to it, like in that book about the kids on the desert island. I don't remember the name.

Gan touches my body. Down there. I grab his shoulders and shake him once, lightly. His head rocks back on his neck. His eyes all wide.

"Cut it out with that gay shit," I say.

"But I thought—"

"This is different."

He is quiet. I shut off the water. I towel him off. I dry myself and him, watching in the mirror. Only, sometimes he's looking at himself, sometimes he's looking at me.

"Go get me some water," I say.

"Okay," he says.

I may have given the wrong impression about Mason. He doesn't just deal in boys and the occasional thirty-one year old who doesn't pay him back. He's got lots of things going on. Worldwide, too. It's just that most of the other guys he can't trust with the kids. They have families, some of them. A few kids of their own. The Union would look down on that. If they knew. If there was one. I mean, he's a sick fuck. But he's not completely sick, if you know what I mean. No. He's got girls, and houses full of women, and animals, too, for the really out there ones.

It's just that, here in America? He makes most of his money off little boys. I don't know what that says about America, or the guys with money who live and work here. All I know is that, when I'm going overseas? It's almost never to bring back one that Paris gets.

See, he's got this guy works for him. Twenty-two, twenty-three, maybe. I don't keep up with it. He's young, though. Sharp face. Blonde hair neatly combed in whatever the latest MTV style is. Mason calls him 'my little fisherman'. That's what he does. Mason gives him two, three grand sometimes, and ships him off to New York or Atlanta, Chicago, you name it. He goes and hangs out at bus stations, arcades, gets to know people who work in orphanages. The bastard calls it 'window shopping'.

He's looking for what they both call 'new merchandise'.

I met him a few times, bringing one back that he got. He told me that sometimes they are already hustling. So Jimmy Paris takes them back to his hotel, shows them a good time, pays them and as they are leaving out the side door he says to them 'Hey. Wanna make some real money?' and then he gives them the spiel. Rich old men, wonderful places to live, you know. The works. The ones who don't hustle already, though, those are a bit tougher. Not much, though.

He said he likes those best. 'It's like a game' he said, 'like when you were little'. I didn't know what he was talking about. I never played games like that when I was a kid. I know what he means, but that was never a game. Still isn't, really. Not with the way he does it, or what happens to them after. But to him it is. Like I said, you've got to love your job if you're going to be good at it.

Gan's standing in the doorway. Glass in his hand. Pitcher in the other. He pours water into the glass as I'm toweling off.

"Guy ever come to the place you were named Paris?"

"Huh?" he asks, stopping.

I slide into my pants; left leg, then right one.

"Did a guy ever come to you, you know. When you worked there. Guy named Paris."

He looks down, "I dunno. I never asked names," long pause, "Why?"

"Bout this tall," I said, gesturing, "blonde. Pretty."

"A few were like that. Mostly from across the border."

I walk to him. I don't look in the mirror. I never look in mirrors. I set the pitcher down. I set the glass to the side. I tilt his chin up.

"I'm not taking you to Mason."

His eyes sparkle.

"What?"

"I said, I'm not taking you to Mason."

"Okay," he says, smiling.

I walk past him into the room. Undershirt; right arm then left.

"Wait, but won't he be mad?"

Gun belt; Right shoulder, then left. Ease Virginia and Wolf home. Pull a little bit up, then ease them back again.

"Yeah."

"Will he send someone after us?"

"Yes."

I hear the springs on the bed groan. I look back over my shoulder and he's sitting on the bed, head in hands.

"Will they kill you?"

"They'll try."

"Then we can't. I mean, you can't."

Turning around, I say "I have an idea."

"What is it?" he asks, turning his head up to me. The light from the bathroom slides across his face just right. Before I can stop myself, my hand touches his cheek.

"Stay here," I say and walk toward the door.

"Tell me what it is," he says standing.

I turn and put that expression on my face. I see his eyes change size, "I said, stay here. I mean it. Lock the door. No one gets in here but me. No one," I say and I open and close the door. I wait a second until I hear it lock. This whole thing sounds like some cheesy Hollywood scene. I hear him lean against the door. I hear him start to cry.

I walk down the hall.

18 • Bygones

S EE, WHAT I leave out all the time is talking about how Gan wasn't the first one. I wish he was. Okay? There. I said it. I wish he was.

I had just done a job for this sick fuck named Maldone. Like to have guys who looked at his wife offed one finger at a time. Real piece of work, this guy. So he has me get rid of one and bring him the guy's left thumb.

So I walk in to bring him the thumb. He's got a big fat envelope (only, he's one of those guys that says 'ahn-vel-ope', and I hate that) on the desk when I come in. Only, he ain't there. The girl who answered the door, she says I'm just supposed to leave the package and take the envelope. Ahnvelope. Whatever. But I explain to her that he specified that I was supposed to deliver the finger to him directly. She keeps explaining that he said I was to leave it on the desk and take the money and I ask her "Where is he?"

"He's indisposed" She says.

"Oh, really?" I say

"Yes, sir. Now, if you'll please—"

So I brush past her and start toward the stairs. I've done this job long enough to know what that word means. Indisposed. In-des-posed. Whatever.

She's squawking at me the whole time I'm going up the steps. But I was told to deliver the thumb directly to him. I never change anything on a contract. Guy says to deliver it to him, I deliver it to him only. So I'm climbing steps and as I get to the top, I see that one of the doors is slightly open.

I walk around the curve and go to rap on the door with my knuckle, only it was more open than I thought. It swings wide. And I see it. What's happening. Maldone sitting on the bed and this little ass between his legs, a little head bobbing up and down over his crotch.

This sick bastard doesn't even stop. The boy tries to, but Maldone keeps pushing his head up and down and looks right at me, smiling.

It's the slurping sounds I remember. I'm sick to my stomach when I do.

"Ah. Zeus. What a pleasant surprise," he says, like something out of a movie.

"Yeah. Whatever. I have what you asked for," I say. Only, I notice something going on downstairs. I'm waking up down there. I'm liking this, the awkwardness of the moment as it stretches between us. I want to tell him to stop. To let the boy alone. To shoot his cheap movie grin.

But I don't.

"May I see it?" he says, holding out his other hand. I start to wonder how long the kid's been at this. I wonder if he means in front of the kid. I take out the little wooden box he told me to put it in. To this day, I have no idea how, but it was just exactly big enough for the finger.

I have to walk closer to the bed to hand it to him. As I do, the kids eyes roll to the side so he can look at me while he's doing it. That makes my stomach turn over. But I'm rock hard because of it. I want to look away, but Maldone is looking at my eyes. It's a stare down: who'll look away first. You don't ever let it be you. Not in my business.

He slides the cover open and inhales sharp. He tosses his head back and goes rigid. The slurping sounds get worse. I'm about to vomit. But my heart is beating at my insides like it wants out. I'm standing stone. I don't even blink. The kid is watching me the whole time.

I don't remember much else of what happened that day. I got my money and left. I thought I saw that kid on a milk carton a few weeks later. I hope he lived.

I doubt he did.

19 • Boys for the Bonfire

THERE'S THAT BOOK by that Russian guy. The one about the Brit who wants the little American girl. I forget the name. There's a big deal about that book, but so what? It's a little girl. Find me a father anywhere who hasn't had impure thoughts about his skinned-knee, scraped-shin daughter or her prim little girlfriends in grade seven and I'll show you a man who'd have preferred a son, but with the same result. The reason people get outraged about a book is simple: it's always something about real life that enters into something that's supposed to be totally about escape.

Take that book, for example. I find it in just about every house I go into, as a guest or not. It's a good book as far as it goes. It's obvious the main character is snowjobbing the reader, though. Worse, he tells you he is. Something like that, you have to read against the grain. I'm sure in every class they teach that book, there's some girl who sits up and raves about how she likes the main character. She thinks he's charismatic and funny. Only, I've met those guys. Put bullets in them. You get to know someone pretty intimately when you're about to shoot them. Or bring them the next snack for their huge sex appetite. I imagine that a few people, though, get it. See what that character is. Get pissed off.

Problem is, lots of guys write lots of books about that same thing. Always much more shocking if you wake up and realize what you're reading. That book about the kids on the island. Same thing, only boys, and instead of the guy molesting them, it's nature itself. See, but no one gets all up in arms over that one because it's little boys. What gets me is, in all these books I take and read, people *want* a little boy to suffer. They want him to be vulnerable and confused and trapped in the snow with only his dog to save him. They want him on that island, naked, covered in war paint. Books like that are called 'beautiful' and 'haunting'.

I'm thinking about all this as the elevator is taking a millennium to reach the ground floor.

I'm checking and re-checking the clip and action.

If someone were ever to write a book like that Russian guy wrote, only where a guy does the same thing, but to a little boy, on the front cover they'd say 'haunting' or 'a heartbreaking coming of age tale'. Let someone write it about a little girl, though, and it's pornography.

I'm checking the springs in the holsters.

It seems almost like America wants their boys hurt. That they need that. That guy who writes books about the wolf and the boy: every book has a scene where the kid gets caught in an avalanche or a freak blizzard. Invariably, the kid winds up naked and alone and bleeding to death and it's only the effort of the wolf that saves him. The boy can never do it himself. If they did that with a female character in a long set of books like that, the feminists would be up in arms. But does anyone mind it when it's a little boy? They make kids read those books in junior high. They call them Literature. Capital 'L'.

The panel lights up 3. Guns in holsters. Deep breath in. Picture all the black gunk in my muscles being pulled into my lungs.

The panel lights up 2. Feel it pulling from my toes.

The panel lights up 1. I exhale black smoke from my center.

The doors open. The soft ping sound.

I step out.

Wolf in a storm.

20 • Deconstruction Man

S O, WHAT YOU'RE SAYING is that it's your job to look at books and guess what the author wanted you to think about when he wrote it?" I asked the man. I remember I was pretty interested in what he had to say, so I took the gun out of his mouth.

He reached up and rubbed his jaw with his right hand and smacked his lips a few times. They always do that. Having a gun in your mouth isn't very comfortable.

"Not really, but that's close," he said, not looking up at me.

"Why don't you just ask the guy who wrote it?" I asked, resting my elbows on my knees and leaning forward.

His name was James Black. He was a professor at the college. His students called him Jim. Lots of other things behind his back, too. He looked like one of those fast food mascot characters, sitting there on his knees. I couldn't decide which.

"It's not that simple," he said, still afraid I'd shoot him if I didn't like his answer.

I bet his students would be wetting themselves if they could see him like this.

"Then dumb it down for me."

"Deconstruction is where you take a book apart piece by piece. All good fiction is written in layers, you see. It's up to the author to provide all levels of meaning for the work. At least, in the modern aesthetic it is," he said.

"And these guys, these moderns, they wanted what again?" I asked

"They wanted to make books more difficult to read. The idea was art for art's sake."

"Like the guy with the crucifix in a jar of piss."

"Something like that, yeah. That's a different movement, though."

I shook my head.

"Are you going to kill me?" he asked from under his eyebrows.

"Do you have 45 grand to pay me, in cash, right now?" I asked back.

He didn't say anything.

"So you pull apart these books for the pieces, these layers, you said. Then what?" I ask.

"Why should I tell you anything," he says, turning his head to the side. I've seen kids do this routine.

"Aren't you a professor?"

He looked up at me when I said that, but slowly.

"Aren't you a teacher?"

He nodded his head up and down just a little.

"Then shouldn't you want to teach me something?" I reached over on the desk and pulled the book I'd taken off his shelf to me, "This one. Did you deconstruct it?" I ask.

He nods again.

"What are the layers?"

And he starts explaining about how the man lost on an island is a metaphor for all of us. How we're all lost in our society. He tells me to look at certain pages and I do. I read what he tells me to. He keeps going on, though, that there's this whole other thing happening underneath even that. About how we're all just plain lost, each one of us.

And I shot him. I had to. That's my job. But I think he was happy that he finally got what he wanted.

A student that listened.

A guy once told me that there are these riddle puzzle poems in Buddhism called Koans before I offed him. He said that they were meant to make a student think on a new level, to discover the world with your real eyes. The most famous one is where the master asks the student "When you think, who is thinking?" The one I memorized, though, says that if you should see the Buddha coming along the road?

Kill him.

21 • The Levee Breaks

BACK THEN, THOUGH. Back to before all of this.

I had only been gone from the room a few hours back on the second day of the trip when I came back in to find Gan drunk. He was lying on the floor in nothing but his boxer shorts and around him were the remains of everything that had been in the courtesy refrigerator. I closed the door behind me, watching him.

"Oh, zews. Haryuh?" he mumbled, reaching out to me with his arms.

I didn't say anything, walking to the bed and sitting down.

This was before I knew what I was going to do. Before I had any idea what the outcome of the story was going to be.

"Gone asser me?" he said again, dropping his arms with a violent thud, "Oww."

"I'm okay kid. How about you?" I said.

"Figh en dandy as candeee," he said, smiling to himself.

I got up to go run the cold water. Emmaus had had to do this for me several times. I knew the drill by now. Gan was going to hate me. But it was better than waiting it out. I had walked five steps and switched on the lights when he said, "Thass whuh he ussah say, aneehow."

I stopped without turning.

"Who?" I asked, knowing it was a mistake.

"Pariss," he said. In the bathroom mirror I could just see his hand as it came up over the counter carrying an empty bottle and moving it around like kids do with toy spaceships.

I turned and picked him up, walking his entire dead weight to the bathroom.

"Whuh'r you doon?" he asked from over my shoulder, his breath jouncing some with each of my footsteps.

"When did you ever meet Paris?" I asked.

"Fugger," Gan said and stopped wiggling.

I sat him down on the edge of the vanity and started taking his right shoe off.

"When did you meet Paris?"

"Came in suhm. Only wanded me," he said, and I bent back to untying the horrible knot he had put in his laces, when he said, "hurt mee."

I froze.

"Did he?" I asked, concentrating on the knot, not looking up.

"Uh huh." He leaned back too far too fast and there was a thunk as his head hit the mirror, "oww."

"Careful," I said and caught my breath for a minute. What was I saying? What was I asking?

"I alwayz liked the name Pariss. Iz fruhm the war."

"Which war?" I asked, moving over to the left shoe.

"Thuh troe jun un."

I picked Gan up, putting him on his own two feet. I set his shoes side by side just outside the bathroom door, "Strip," I said.

He started to pull his shirt out from his pants, and made a motion with his left heel to toe out of his right shoe, even though they weren't on. He fell backward, misjudging his balance. I watched from the door and he hit, ass first, on the tile. His head hit the cupboard under the bathroom sink. He sat still for a moment.

Then his head began to move up and down and his chest began to shake. He sniffled. When he looked up at me from under his messy hair, I don't know what happened.

"Helb mee," he said, and reached out like an infant. He was sobbing and the tears were running down his cheek. He just kept repeating it over and over again. I stood stock still for a moment. Then I reached out and took his hands. I lifted him up and to me. He wrapped his arms completely around my ribs and back in a bear hug. I couldn't breathe for a second. I could feel his hot cheek through my shirt. "Helb mee. Oh, gawd—helb me" he kept repeating.

He fell asleep that way. That's when I heard the first splash of water going over the side of the tub. I wrapped my arm completely around him and moved us both close enough for me to shut off the tap. I released the stopper. No sense sobering him up, now. I put my other arm under his knees and carried him to the bed. I put him on his side and he curled into a ball quickly.

"Zews?" he asked in a whisper just after I shut off the lamp.

"Yes," I said.

"Done tayk mee bag to Paris."

I was silent.

"He hurrd me bad. Reel bad."

I was silent.

"Zews?"

"Okay. I won't."

He was silent the rest of the night.

22 • Fork in the Road

S I STEP OUT of the elevator, exhaling invisible black smoke, there is a big football-player type standing there. I'm tall. He's taller. He doesn't move. That's fine. Sometimes I prefer it that way.

Emmaus taught me something a long time ago and it still holds true today: men are essentially afraid of other men. That's why guns. That's why sports. Women dress to impress other women, and men get musclebound to convince other men not to attack them.

So I attack. The important thing is to do it with your energy, not your body. America is like that. You can attack someone with your energy all you want, and that's not a crime. You can leer at their photographs online with a bottle of Suave sitting nearby and no one recognizes that as a crime. But try to put a finger on someone, and you'll do 25 to life in Florida.

At first, I don't think he knows what's happening. Then he feels it. I'm concentrating on him. Fully concentrating. I don't think he's ever had a woman concentrate on him so hard. He steps back haltingly. Then again. His face is still set in the mask of a tough guy, but he's moving. I step forward and still I'm boring into him. It's a laser, and it's dead accurate. He doesn't speak. He doesn't know how to. He just backs up. And that's all I wanted.

Wolves do that all the time.

On the street, it's bright. It's so bright it takes my eyes a minute to adjust, even behind the sunglasses. In that second I'm blinded. I don't like that at all.

Emmaus taught me that, too. One of his favorite games would be to blindfold me, tie me up, and then cut me. Never very big cuts. Just little ones of varying lengths. When the cut was done, he made me tell him exactly where it was on my body, and exactly how long it was. It's called proprioception, he said. I always had to ignore his hitched breath when he did it. I knew it got him off. But I was interested in it for the training.

It's through that same sense, while I'm blinded, that I can tell that Dubois just came out the front door of the hotel across the street. When my glasses adjust, he's there. He doesn't recognize me, now that I've got hardly any hair. Concentrating on the cars as I step into the street, I follow. They slowly glide to a stop. I don't want them screeching. That'll make him look.

I want this to happen quickly. Very little mess.

I'm hoping he feels the same deep down.

Because some men do give up. Some guys, you walk up on them, and they almost thank you. Life is some pretty rank and foul shit sometimes. Some guys find ways to do themselves that don't look like suicide. Some guys think of me as a savior.

Dubois is moving fast along the street. He's good at weaving in and out of people. I'm better. In just a few strides I'm right behind him when he stops. I'm shocked because I didn't feel that coming. Normally, I would have.

He stops dead in his tracks and turns around as though he's forgotten something back in his room. I learned all about this. This is Chinese Assassin stuff. As he turns, I turn around him at exactly his speed. If you pay attention, you can always tell where someone is going to turn next.

Only, he doesn't turn around. He starts back up the street we just came from. And he's moving. We come back to the front door of the Hotel he's staying in and he goes in the front door. The reflection in the polished glass is of the Hotel I'm staying in. And that's when I see her.

As Dubois goes into the lobby, the door in my hand, I see Leeda walking into the lobby of the Hotel I'm staying in. In the flash of her coat and the glint off the glass of the door, I can see:

She's got a gun under her jacket.

23 • Daddy and the Shovel

I REMEMBER THE sound most of all. Dirt being cut into by an edge. The rasp of something again and again slicing into dirt. And sobbing.

I didn't look down in the hole because I knew who was in it. I knew he was down there. All I did was keep putting the shovel into the dirt, then dumping it over the side. After awhile of doing this, my back didn't hurt anymore. It went beyond the hurting. I wasn't me. I was somewhere else watching, like a TV that I couldn't shut off or mute.

"You keep on shoveling boy," was all I heard.

Emmaus sitting off to the side. He had his gun resting on his lap. His eyes were steady on me. He refused to move them, or even to blink.

In the hole was a boy not that much older than me. I knew that. I wouldn't look down into the hole at him. I knew if I did, he'd be looking back up at me. He'd be blinking every time a shovel full of dirt hit him to keep it out of his eyes. Only, he wouldn't be able to do that forever. Eventually, there'd be too much dirt. I knew that he was struggling with the ropes that had his hands tied to his chest. Working his jaw against the cheap bandana that was knotted in his mouth, trying to scream.

I kept shoveling. I had to.

"Few more of these jobs and you'll be big in the shoulders," Emmaus said.

I had to because I told him that I wanted to know what it was like to kill someone. To end them. To stop them. His lips pulled back from his teeth in a grimace when I'd asked. To this day, I don't know if that was pleasure or pain. Maybe both. He'd agreed, but he got to choose who and how.

This poor kid was just some two-bit junky. He told everyone he was straight, but sucked guys off for skag. Only, when they stopped giving it to him that way, he started having to pay like everyone else. And he started owing money. And then he couldn't pay it back. Someone called someone else, who called a friend of his, and suddenly here we are: two fifteen a.m. on a Wednesday burying the kid alive in the middle of a plot where they're building a high rise.

And I can't help but think that this kid is someone's son. That he has a dad who maybe always wanted to get off work early on Friday's, take him to a baseball game. Who kissed a girl in seventh grade and got his first hard on. And he wasn't that much older than me. And he was lying in a pit six foot below me trying to scream for help while some kid buried him alive trying to impress a paid killer.

After that was done, Emmaus had taken me back to the hotel and made me shower. And I cried. I don't tell people that part, but I cried like a girl in the shower. And I thought I hid it pretty well, only he knew. I came out with my breath still catching. I sat down on the bed. He moved up beside me and I felt his arm move around behind my back. And I wanted nothing more at that moment than for him to put his arm around my shoulder and pull me to him.

He pulled my hair back until I was lying on the bed and he was over me, his face millimeters from mine.

"Do you see how you feel right now?" he said in that snake hiss of his.

I nodded as much as I could without pulling more of my hair.

"Good. Don't you fucking ever forget it. You kill people. You kill people well. You get paid to kill people well. But don't you ever fucking forget that in that hole is another human being. That you are destroying another person. Don't you ever forget it, not even for a second."

He was more violent with me that night than he had ever been before.

That next day, after the bleeding had stopped, he took me out to a place a friend of his owned. That day, he bought me a gun.

24 • Getting Away

THE ELEVATOR DOOR is just closing on Dubois' face as I walk into the lobby and head for the main desk.

"Telephone," I say.

The girl behind the desk stops chewing bubblegum long enough to not say what she's been taught to say about non guests using the telephone when she looks at me. She sets the telephone up on the desk.

I dial the room.

No answer.

I hang it up. She reaches to take it back. I start dialing again. The front desk of the hotel I'm staying at answers.

"Listen, I'm in room 2440. I left my son alone in there and I'm worried about him. Can you go up and check on him for me?" I say. I swear, I should get an academy award for sounding like some dead-beat banker who had to drag junior off on a trip with him because the wife decided to go to Barbados for the week. I should win an award for not sounding as concerned as I am.

"I'm sorry, sir, it is not our policy to—"

"Go up to room 2440 and knock on the door. Now. I'll wait."

"I'm terribly sorry sir, but—"

I slam the phone down.

Every man makes choices in his life. This is one in front of me right now.

I've always been one to know what he's doing before he does it. When I step out the door to go on a job, I know where I'm going and why I'm going there long before I even get within a mile of either of those things. But now there's Gan. And Leeda. And a gun.

25 • The Big Reveal

TRAFFIC STOPS FOR me. That's another one of those things that Emmaus taught me. You can make anyone stop for you or move out of your way. Size isn't just a flesh thing. People perceive with other senses all the time. All you have to know is what to do to make yourself bigger. I do.

Sliding through the door. I have my hand on Virginia. She's a quiet girl, even in a big echo room like this. I wonder just how good a shot Leeda is.

She's not anywhere in the lobby. I can tell, because none of my neck hairs stand on end.

The elevator button lights up. Normally, going to a job, I take the stairs. But I need to get there fast. She must already be halfway there. One of the reasons that rich people choose the penthouse is that it takes a bit of time to get there. Ideally, you're supposed to sign in as a guest downstairs. That gives the person behind the counter time enough to ring up and tell the people upstairs someone is on the way up. Just time enough to get the prostitute out the back way or put the spoon somewhere so no one can see the burn mark on the bottom.

I choose it because it's high ground.

Anyone in the military will tell you that's just a good idea: camp on high ground.

The elevator opens and there must be about thirty people inside. Some convention or something. They all look alike. They take their own sweet time filing out, talking the entire time about whatever they're here for. I try to keep my cool, but I grab the last one by the elbow and move him out of my way.

"Hey, pal, watch it—" he says.

I use my grip on his arm to spin myself into the elevator and press the top floor and the button marked 'door close' at the same time. Some woman is walking from the front door very quickly.

"Hold the elevator, please," she's saying.

The doors are sliding closed.

"Hold the elevator, please!" She's saying.

The doors are sliding closed.

She looks kind of like Sigourney Weaver.

"HOLD THE—" She yells, breaking into a trot.

The doors close.

When they open again, I'm trying my best to dodge the panic that's wiggling inside me, threatening to burst out. Emmaus always said that this would happen someday; that the fear would come wriggling up. I never believed him.

Until today, it's never happened.

Immediately to the left, I see the door is still closed.

Virginia and Wolf leap into my hands. Wolf knows the routine, so he's pointed to the door on the right, while Virginia is pointed at the door to the room Gan and I are staying in. I'm somewhere between.

When we reach the door, I push on it with Virginia's mouth. Just like I thought, it swings open. Nothing seems to be wrong in the outer room. I walk through the next room. The television is still on. Some religious program. I guarantee Gan wasn't watching that. I stop.

The bedroom door is open just a little. I'd closed it when I left. Wolf is pointed back toward the door, watching behind me. Virginia presses on the bedroom door and it creaks open. The indentation on the bed where he had been sleeping hasn't had time to straighten out. The shower is running.

I just keep repeating the word 'please' in my head without knowing who I'm asking, or what for. I walk around the corner quickly. Some part of my brain is chastising me for having my guns down as I step into the bathroom. The voice sounds just like Emmaus.

The water is just running into an empty tub.

Gan isn't here.

On the mirror is written, in dark purple lipstick: 'You get him back when we get Jimmy'

She means Dubois. She doesn't know that.

There's a lot of things she doesn't know.

I'm already back at the elevator before the water finishes running out of the tub drain back in the room.

26 • The Stories that Get Around

ONE OF THE very first gigs I soloed on was this rock star. Big round glasses that made him look like a fly. It was a shame for me, too. I'd always liked the guy's music. Emmaus never let me listen to anything but classical. Well, what I call classical, anyway. He knew the different names for the different decades and styles. I really didn't care. There were no words to it. Shit always put me to sleep anyway.

But this guy's band got big. Very big. You couldn't turn on the television without seeing him somewhere. He had these lips you couldn't help but notice. Not big or thick, just you couldn't help but notice them.

I threatened the kid at the backstage door to get into the dressing room. I always thought of it like that. That was something I'd always done, even before Emmaus came along. You do your best to think of someone as younger, less intelligent—anything you can to make yourself feel superior. That way no matter what you do, you're always in control. When you're just a kid on the streets doing whatever comes along for money, that's very helpful.

So I'm in the guy's dressing room. Huge mirrors. Dish full of candy, all of it blue in color. I couldn't help but shake my head. The stories are always true about stuff like that.

The place is shaped like an 'L'. Around the corner, there's the sound of a shower running. Someone is singing warm up scales. I take a handful of the little chocolate covered blue candies, and sit down in the overstuffed armchair. It's very comfortable.

When he comes out of the shower, he's not wearing anything.

I notice right off that some of the other stories about this guy are true, too.

I can't tell what he's more shocked at; me sitting here, or Virginia pointed at him.

I imagine it's all the same thing.

He starts shaking.

"Who the f—" he starts, just getting into that 'f' sound. I raised my hand and he stopped talking.

"I think you know who I am," I say. I got off on saying it like that when I was younger. It always sounded like some really great movie. I don't let him finish, because that particular 'f' word gives people power. If you let them start saying it, it somehow gives power. It's become almost a Mantra. I never let anyone finish it, anymore.

"What the f—" he starts, again.

"I think you know what I want," I say. I said that a lot, too.

He pauses. It's probably just then that he realizes I haven't blinked since he came around the corner.

"Let me get a towel, and—" he starts.

"No," I say.

"Who sent you?" he asks.

"Who do you think?" I ask back. It's like a thing cats do with crickets. I'm just batting him around a little. I want him to fully realize what's going on before we really start to talk. Judging from how much he's shrunk up, I'm guessing we're almost there.

"Is this about that girl back in Houston? Cause I had no idea she had taken that much, man, and I don't know where they dumped her, either, so you can—" I let him go on for a second, thinking he's gotten the control back.

"This has nothing to do with her." Best never to let them know you don't have any idea what they are talking about. Emmaus taught me a few pat answers to things like that when they come up. This is the one that usually works best. Makes them think you've been watching for a while. That you have all kinds of information.

"What's it about, then?" he asks. There we are. Go time.

"Do you know who Mason is?" I ask.

It takes him a second. He'd probably know Jimmy Paris, more. That's who usually delivers if it isn't me. After a moment, though, it registers. He shrinks up all the way. His arms start to shake a bit. He bites his lip.

"I can see that you do. Good. He, of course, remembers you," I say.

I let that sink in for a second.

There's a knock at the door.

"Five minutes," someone says.

Mr. Rockstar doesn't say anything.

I still haven't blinked.

"Look, you gotta believe me. I had no idea they were all going to go after the kid like that. I tried to stop them, I swear—"

"That's not my problem," I say.

"I didn't know that they did it, though, or how much they'd given him—"

"Again, not my problem. What you do with the merchandise once it's delivered has nothing to do with me."

"I can ask, you know—maybe they remember where they dumped the body or whatever—" He's really shaking good now. Goosebumps all up and down his chest and stomach.

"Ah, now we reach the part that IS my problem. You see, you didn't purchase that particular piece. Your contract *specifically* said your intention was to rent. Rented. That means that the merchandise in question is to be returned to the proper owner in roughly the same condition it was given to you," I say, let that sink in.

"Oh, shit, man, I know—I know—but it's not my fault—I had to go on stage and I didn't know that the road crew was going to—"

"Now we're getting back into the area that's not my problem. That's not good. See, we can do this the easy way, or we can do this a way that requires a bit more work on my part. Either way is okay with me, but I'm assuming you'd like to have me do this easy," I said.

"What's that mean?" he asks. Good. I've got him back in the moment.

"Regardless of what happened to the merchandise when it was in your care, that particular piece was not returned to Mr. Mason at all. That was two weeks ago. Mr. Mason, being a forgiving man, allowed you a week to attempt to explain and make amends. He likes you, you see," I say, standing up.

He moves backward as far as he can until he's against the mirror. Both of him are standing back to back watching me.

"So, you have one of two choices. Either you can hand over the merchandise with a small late fee, or—" I let that trail off, taking another step closer.

"Or what?" he asks. Or, that's what I'm gonna assume he asks. Most of the time, at this point, what the movie guys call 'The Big Reveal' part, they are too scared to make a whole lot of sense. He hasn't wet himself, though. That's a good thing. He's still coherent.

"Or I have to find a way to get satisfactory payment from you to compensate Mr. Mason on the loss of a very valuable piece of equipment," I answer. In a movie, this would be a big music cue.

He gulps, "And—umm—and what would—uh—"

"I don't know yet. That's up to you to decide." This isn't true. I have very specific instructions, but I like to make them think they have a way out. It's part of the game.

He stands up a bit straighter. He starts to step forward.

"I can get anything, man. They love me. Anything. What do you want?"

I hold my hand up to stop him. His eyes lose all the ground they just gained. He steps backward.

"It's not a matter of what I want. It's about what Mr. Mason feels would be fair. I'm assuming, then, that you do not have the merchandise to turn over in any condition?" I used to love talking like this. It made me feel like I was in one of those court dramas.

He shakes his head from side to side.

I cock my head a bit to the left, "That's unfortunate."

I reach into my pocket. This would be another music cue.

"Your family is from Greenville, right? That's where you grew up?" I ask him.

This catches him so off guard he doesn't know how to answer.

"Did you, or did you not, grow up in Greenville?" I ask.

He nods.

I nod, too. I take the three photographs from out of my pocket. I flip through them idly, "Nice place to grow up in?" I ask. He'll say yes, he guesses, but I was just there a few hours ago. It's a rathole. Most little towns like that are. People don't live there, they get trapped there.

"Yeah, I guess," he says.

In my head, this would make a great movie. I flip the photos around so that he can see them. At first he says nothing, then he almost reaches for them. Then his eyes get all wet and shiny. His lip starts to shake. There is a knock at the door.

"Three minutes."

"No," he says.

"Yes," I say.

"No," he says, closing his eyes.

"You see, this is the payment that Mr. Mason considered fair. An even exchange," I say, still holding the photos level.

"But—but he's only twelve—" Mr. Rockstar is saying, with his eyes closed.

"Mr. Mason had three good years of service from the particular piece of merchandise he rented to you. So, in exchange, we will extract three years of service from a similar piece which was, I believe, related to you?"

"He's only twelve—" Mr. Rockstar keeps repeating.

"Again, we're getting into an area that is *not* my problem."

"Please, no—anything, but please no—" Mr. Rockstar is saying over and over again.

"Mr. Mason assures you that most of his clientele, *unlike* you, do not damage the goods beyond a reasonable amount of wear and tear. Your property will be cared for quite well, and will be returned to you in three years time, after it has worked off the remainder of what would have been considered the 'earning lifespan' of the other unit."

"No—please—I'll do anything—"

There is a knock at the door.

"One minute."

I set the photographs on the table next to him. I walk toward the door.

From behind me, he says, "I'll go to the police."

I stop.

Over my shoulder, without turning, I say, "And ruin your precious reputation? Prove all the stories going around about you are right?"

I don't look back at him. I don't have to. I know what he'll do: Check every milk carton he comes across for a picture that looks like his little boy until, one day, he finds it. I wonder, as I'm walking out the back way, listening to the roaring crowd above, what will be worse for him. Seeing that picture on a milk carton, or knowing that his boy isn't missing at all.

27 • The Stranger

THE PROFESSOR I took care of a while back told me about all kinds of books. One he talked to me about was by some guy named Camus. You don't say that 'cam-us', though; it's 'cam-oo'. I couldn't help but laugh at that when he said it.

In that book, there was this guy who shot some Arab just because. I mean, the sun and the fatigue got in his eyes, or whatever. Point is, though, that the other guy really wasn't doing anything. That's not what's important about the book.

The professor says that the book is important because the main character doesn't feel any emotion. He's just as upset about his mother dying as he is about being in jail. He doesn't care one way or the other. I had to think about that for a while. The professor said what's important about the book is that the character is more disinterested in his own life than the person who is reading it.

I asked him where his copy of that book was, and he said he didn't have one. It was something he'd read when he was a student. I asked him why, if he took all the time and trouble to read a book, he didn't keep a copy around to read again or whatever. He said he didn't know, that the thought had never really occurred to him.

After I took care of him, I spent a long time just wandering around looking at his books. I picked a few out that I thought looked like good ones. He was right, though. No copy of this book by Camus. Cam-oo.

When I left there I went to this bookstore. It felt weird walking into a bookstore with guns. It was so bright and the carpet was nice. It was like a hotel lobby, only I didn't know how to act there. I found some kid walking around with a nametag on. That was a little weird, too. Here was a kid about the same age as the ones I was used to dealing with. He knew where books were and what they were about. Not like the professor, no, but when I worked up enough stroke to ask him about the book, he knew it.

"Oh, yeah. I read that one. Good book. I didn't like the ending, though," the kid says, walking me to where the section is.

"What was wrong with the ending?" I asked him.

"I dunno. It was really anticlimactic, in a way."

When I looked that up later, I found out that he meant it didn't get the job done. I knew all about that feeling.

So I read the book cover to cover sitting in my car right outside. The only time I stopped was to watch that kid walk to his car when his shift was over. Some late model import piece of shit. I bet he was paid for it with that job. I watched it until the taillights disappeared down the main road. Then I went back to reading.

The book wasn't that confusing. I thought it would be. But after I got to a certain point and it was still really easy and sort of boring, I figured out there must be something else going on. Like, underneath or whatever. As I finished the rest of it, I started to think about each sentence. That's when I got it.

This guy had no past.

So I put the book in the glove compartment of the car I had at the time. Then I got on the interstate and drove out to the suburbs. I wove through the streets without even thinking.

I pulled up in front of the house and shut the engine off.

I was wondering if the old couple still lived there.

See, kids can be given up for adoption for just about any reason. No one really looks into why. At just about any age, too. People do that with pets all the time. Just don't want it anymore, so they give it up for someone else to deal with. Trash is like that; you walk a bag to the corner at night and in the morning, the bag isn't there. It's not your problem anymore.

I could pretend to hate them. That's how I was supposed to feel, I guess. But truthfully, what made me drive out here? I didn't feel anything. I never knew enough about them to hate them.

The homes that came after that? Oh, I had plenty of hate for those guys. Waking up to a hand down your pants will do that to you. But this house? This was just another house on another street in anywhere.

I started the car and left.

28 • Frog and Scorpion

I HAD NO idea where Dubois was by now, but I knew he wouldn't be leaving town, yet. He thought he was safe here. This meant I had to get into his room. I've had to do that before. I just hate the extra steps involved. It gets sort of boring after a while.

Backdoor. Knock. "Delivery." Door opens. Gun in face. "I need you to tell me what room someone is in and get me a key. Do that and you live, got it?" He nods slow. Walk through the hallway. Waiting just around the corner as the kid checks the registry, and grabs the key. Minor irritation as the head whateverthehelltheycallthem asks 'what are you doing?' Kid gives a lame excuse, brings me the room number and the key. No words, but he agrees not to say anything or else.

The elevator is playing some song that I recognize. A version of something I've heard a million times before, but I can't think of it. I hate that. The ding of the doors opening is almost exactly on the beat.

Down the hallway. The floor Dubois chose is 14. That means it's really the thirteenth floor. They number them that way. Skip thirteen. Silly. Only, I guess for Dubois, it isn't.

I put the key in the lock and walk in.

The room smells like cinnamon. Housekeeping has been in since he left, then. I close the door behind me and flick on the light. Dull, yellow hotel light. Two beds, round table near the window with two chairs. The usuals. No suitcases. Any clothes Dubois has will be on his back. He didn't escape that long ago. I pull out Wolf and set him on the table. I sit down in the chair.

I think back to that book by Camus. How he wrote it in what he called 'the American style'. To him that meant everything was in these short, declarative sentences. I think about how true that is. How that's how people in America really think. That book about the guy and the little girl talked about it, too. How some agent the Russian guy who wrote it had taken the book to wanted it to be more like that. Short declarative sentences. I wait for Dubois.

The professor had also said that there were no accidents in books. Everything was on purpose. I had never thought about that until then. I see it now. I don't think there are any accidents in life, either. Some guy said that. Some psychologist guy.

There is a click as another key slides into the lock.

I pick up Wolf.

The door opens.

"Did I leave the light on, again?" Someone whispers to himself, then stops short.

"Come in. Close the door," I say.

Dubois looks back out into the hall for a second, hand still on the knob.

"Don't," is all I say.

His chin dips a little toward his chest and he steps inside. He closes the door behind him. I can't see his eyes as he walks over toward the table. He pulls out a chair and sits down hard, exhaling.

We sit silent for a minute.

"I won't go back." He says, "I'll make you kill me."

Lots of guys say that. None of them really mean it. Something about being a person; if there is a chance of living through something horrible, no matter how remote that chance is, they'll take it. Pain is easy, death isn't.

"Not yet," I say.

"What?" he asks, looking up.

"I've been thinking about this. I need you to do something. You need me to do something."

"What do you mean?"

"You need to get away."

"Yes."

"You can't do that on your own."

"I could, maybe, I think—"

All I do is shake my head. He stops talking.

"What is it you need?" he asks.

"That's really none of your business," I say. I let that sink in. I let him remember who has the gun.

"Here's what's going to happen. I'm going to walk out the front door with you. We're going to go across the street. I'm going to make a phone call. Then we're going to take a little drive."

He looks down at his feet.

"At the end of that drive, one of two things is going to happen."

He looks up at me. Our eyes slam into each other.

"Either I walk all three of us out."

"All three of us?" he asks. I don't say anything.

He waits, "Or?"

"I turn you back over to them and walk away."

His eyes shift to the side. His lips go thin. His eyes look wet.

"But if I can't get all three of us out," I say, "I'm going to do something for you that I wouldn't do for anyone else."

"What's that?" he asks.

"I'll shoot you in the head," I say.

His lip starts quivering.

"I'll make sure to kill you if I can't get you out."

He nods slowly. I stand up, and so does he.

Together, we walk toward the door.

29 • Changes

WHEN AN INSECT doesn't change much from the form it's born in to the form it has as an adult, they call that *incomplete* metamorphosis. When they change a lot, like a maggot to a fly, or a caterpillar to a butterfly, that's called *complete*.

I don't know any stories from when I was little. People who work with orphans are of two types. Either giving and nurturing, or that other kind. Other people I meet, they have lots of stories. They know about reading by age whatever. They know about treehouses. What do I know about being little? You don't want me to tell you.

So what I wonder is, if a fly had a mirror, would it look at itself and remember what it looked like when it was little? See, back then it was completely defenseless. It was abandoned. The fly could look in the mirror as an adult, though, and say 'Yeah, I eat shit, but I can fly.'

As we're passing out of the hotel lobby, I catch sight of myself in the glass of the door. This is what I'm thinking.

30 • The Barrel of a Gun

S HOULDN'T I PAY the bill?" Dubois is asking me.

That's an interesting question. Of all the times I've stormed into someone's hotel room and axed them, I've never once thought about the hotel getting stiffed for the money of a few nights stay.

"No," is all I say.

Virginia and Wolf are both under my hands. Dubois is just walking. This is usually the part where they try to make a break for it. Crowded street. Death march. Who wouldn't try? What've you got to lose?

The funny part is this: Just like any hijacker will tell you, if he makes it out alive: people always try to remain calm. They don't try to escape. It's spooky to me sometimes. You hold a gun to someone's head and tell them you're about to shoot them and they just get quiet and still. Some even smile. Guys walking from death row to the chair are usually cool as cucumbers. When I first started out, it made my skin gooseprickle.

We cross over the street. In through the doors of the hotel where I'm staying. Try not to look at my reflection in the glass.

Dubois pushes the button for the elevator.

When the doors open, it's empty. No one else is waiting.

The doors close.

'The Girl from Epenema' is playing. On the real song, that girls voice was always spooky to me. I stop myself before I can remember the first time I heard that song. I don't want to go there. Dubois is shaking.

"Calm down," I say.

He doesn't hear me.

The Elevator stops. The doors open. A woman gets on with a little girl in tow. They both have matching bows in their hair. The doors close. The little girl is standing on the other side of her mother. Just before I look away from them, the little girl peeks from around her mother's leg at me, then hides again. Kids do that.

Without realizing it, I pull back and then slowly peek around again. She does too, gasping and hiding her face against her mother's leg. The elevator stops. The doors open. The woman and the little girl get off. The doors close.

When the elevator stops again, it's the top floor. Dubois steps out and waits.

"Left," I say.

The door to the penthouse on the right is open a little. I can almost see someone, just an outline of an arm and a leg, around a corner into another room. I unlock my door and let Dubois in. I lock the door back behind us. He walks over to the large couch and sits down.

"Mason paying for this?"

I feel like there's something I should be doing other than making this phone call. I walk over to the phone and pick it up off the cradle. I tap the 'on' button. I walk back into the bedroom and then to the mirror. I dial the number written in lipstick.

It rings three times before, "Hello?"

It's her.

"I've got him," I say.

"Good, I was hoping you—" She starts to say.

"Cut the bullshit. Where do we meet?"

"You can't take control this time, Zeus. For trying, the punishment is this." And she hung up.

What I feel like is throwing the phone across the room. What I feel like is pouring bullets into everyone in the hotel. What I feel like is exploding like a nuclear bomb and taking half the civilized world with me.

I dial the number again. There is no answer.

I walk over to my bag. I take out a small tape recorder. Don't ask what Mason usually wants me to tape record. I walk with it to the couch. I throw it into Dubois lap.

He looks up at me.

"If I can't get you out—either way, Mason gets his, understand? Just like in the movies," I say.

Dubois nods. He stands up and walks into the kitchen. He slides the rolling door closed. He's already talking into the microphone.

I dial the number again. There is no answer.

She dies, either way.

I can hear Dubois talking, even with the door to the kitchen closed. Will it be enough? Probably not. But it might get someone looking in the right direction.

There is a knock at the door. That's when the feeling I've been having becomes clear. I was distracted by trying to make the phone call. Virginia goes in one hand, Wolf in the other. Both go behind my back. From the front, I look like a proper Gentleman. From the back, the picture is different.

"Who is it?" I ask through the door.

"Housekeeping."

A man. Heavy set.

"We're okay for today, thank you," I say back.

There is the sound of heavy footsteps shuffling away. The ding of the Elevator. The sound of the doors closing. I unlock the door, and open it, Wolf already coming up.

And I'm looking down the barrel of a gun.

31 • Father Figure

ONE OF THE places I stayed when I was little. Eleven, twelve, I dunno. Foster care, I guess you'd call it. The guy lived alone. I don't know what he told the people to get them to agree to let a boy live with a man who lived alone. He wanted me to take karate. I guess most parents want that for their kids. I've rarely heard of the kid bringing up the idea themselves.

I was only in it for a few weeks before the instructor wanted me to start coming to his house on the weekends for special instruction. That's what he called it. It was mostly hanging out at the local pool. Just me and him. And talking.

It didn't take very long before I was going over to his place and staying the night on weekdays. The guy I was living with didn't care. He preferred it. He kept getting the money to take care of me, only it was the instructor who fed me and made sure I got to school.

And when he started to do stuff to me, I didn't mind. He wasn't the first. I never told him that, though. Why should I? He liked to think he was. Who am I to interrupt his dream, you know? He was good to me. He liked to cuddle a lot, and so what? I was a little kid. Little kids like that shit. He liked to read kids books to me. I liked that. Poetry mostly. Some guy with a bald head and a guitar on the back cover. I liked that.

I guess he was trying to make it like I was really his son.

Only, he and I were having sex. He was one of the type that like to try to make it seem like the kid seduced them. Like the kid was trying to get them in bed. A story about a guy with his head cut off riding through town cutting other people's heads off. Like a little boy who got scared enough, after being read something like that, was also thinking 'this guy's hot. I wonder if he'll do me?' I think what those kind of guys are really doing is trying to get back the little kid that was hurt inside them.

I don't know that I ever had one of those. A kid inside me. If I did, it left a long time ago.

But what do I know?

He had this garden in his backyard. Not like that movie with the old guy from Okinawa. It was a little garden, because that's all he could afford. But it was cool. He had all these special plants, and he knew all the names, all the Latin. He taught me as much of it as he could. How to take care of them. He and I would work on the lessons, then garden. I liked that. We were quiet. Pulling weeds, planting new bulbs, pulling up old plants that had given up. Just moving in and around each other without talking.

He really did teach me martial arts. But that was beside the point. He knew a few different animal styles. Kung fu is what Americans call it. That's not what it's really called, or even what it really means, but ok. That's what he taught me about, mostly. How something whole and amazing in its peace and its violence could become fucked up. We talked about that a lot. He taught me important parts of each of them. He said what was important was not to know one to perfection, but to know important things from each and be able to use them well.

"Bend like tall grass, don't be rigid like Bamboo." When the guy in that movie said something like that all that time later, I laughed. Most people in the theater just nodded their heads like it was sage wisdom they already knew. Only, I did.

He would have kids from his other classes come stay the night with us. They all left with secrets. Only I *lived* in that secret, though. Most dropped out of his class not too long after they came over. A few came back, though, and started doing better in his class. They liked the extra attention. None ever stuck around too long. They'd be paired up with me for sparring and wind up hurt. Then they'd leave.

Almost every night, it was just me and him.

He even let me say no on nights I didn't want to. I liked that.

They picked him up in a patrol car, though. Took him during one of his classes. I'd had a feeling something was going to happen for a long time. One of the kids who'd come to stay one night had cried. He hadn't come back to classes after.

They took him away with handcuffs right in front of his class.

After, they asked me if he'd ever touched me. I told them yeah. What did I know? They made a big fucking deal out of it. I never got to see him again, but if I did, I would have said 'sorry'. Knowing what I know now, it was probably more what I told them than what any of the other kids did that put him away. They started this big investigation into his life. Thing is, they kept calling him horrible. They kept saying he was a monster for what he'd done.

I've seen monsters. I know they exist. Most of them have lawyers good enough that they wouldn't have gone to prison like he did. He fed me three times a day bare minimum. I got whatever type of ice cream I wanted. He read to me all kinds of stuff. He taught me martial arts and self-discipline. Does any of that make it okay that he wanted to have sex with me when I was that young? I don't know. I don't know anything except that they kept calling him a monster, and I wish I could go back there and tell them what I know now.

That monsters exist, but he wasn't one of them.

The guy who was supposed to be taking care of me got investigated, too, and though they found that he wasn't at fault, they kept badgering him all the time about where I was and how I was doing in school. It wasn't too long after that I heard him tell someone on the phone he was mad that he had to start spending money on me again. I wasn't there too long before the lady came with trash bags to put my stuff in. Only, the important things that I was taking away from that time couldn't be put in those bags.

They wouldn't fit.

32 • Showdown

I HEAR THE click before it happens.

It's something I learned a long time ago.

The hammer hitting the striker. I knew it was coming before he did.

So I bent away. I went flat like a table from the waist up.

My arm came up and wrapped around the barrel.

It's so hot it hisses against my skin.

In a moment like that, you don't hear the gunshot; you feel it.

Emmaus didn't teach me that.

I yank the gun to the right. The thumb muscle is nearly the weakest one in the body.

The gun is in his right hand.

The gun is in my left hand.

I grab him by the shirt and fling him into the room. I shut the door. The gun is in my right hand. And pointed at Jimmy Paris.

The kitchen door opens and out comes Dubois.

Without talking I walk over to the television set. I turn it on. I turn to the cable channel that shows all westerns. I turn it up really loud.

Still pointing the gun at Paris, I walk to the wall and pull the picture off. I yank the nail out. I walk to the place where the new hole is.

"Dubois, get this up over the hole. Now," I say.

I walk over and sit down next to Paris.

"How did you do that?" he asks, still so much in shock, he hasn't moved.

I pick him up, and set him against the back of the couch like a doll. I wedge the gun in next to him. Dubois is using the phone to hammer the nail in. I figure we've got about sixty seconds.

"When the door opens," I say, "If you so much as blink Morse Code, I will empty you all over this couch, understand?" I ask.

Paris just nods his head.

On the television, some guy is having a showdown in the middle of an empty street.

Dubois gets the picture on the nail. It just covers the hole in the wall.

There is a knock at the door.

I look at Dubois and then at the door. He moves to it and opens it.

"Is everything alright here, sir? We got a phone call about—" The guy says.

"See?" I say, "I told you it was too loud." I'm looking at Paris.

"Sorry. TV," Dubois says.

I make a show of turning the volume down.

"Oh. Okay. Well, if you guys would—" the guy says.

"No problem," I say.

"Bye now," Dubois says, and closes the door.

If there's one thing you can count on, it's that the people staying below the penthouses always listen for noises upstairs. They want to be the one to tell the newspapers 'I heard the shot and called the police.' I've dealt with that before.

Dubois slumps back against the door. "What the hell happened?" he asks.

I stand up, gun pointed at Paris.

"Who?" I ask. I already know. Who doesn't already know? But I have to hear it.

"Who do you think?" he says back.

I wait a moment, then "Who?"

"Mason. Something about you not delivering a kid he's trying to move," Paris says, looking around. I don't want him getting any ideas. I cock the hammer back. He snaps his attention back to me. Good.

I let a few minutes pass. I dunno what that's called, but it's something Emmaus didn't teach me. I had to learn this on my own. The quiet and the gun work on a guy. Even a hardass like Paris isn't going to be immune to that. So I wait. Even Dubois is just standing there, looking at me. Then at Paris. Then at the gun.

"So, what are you going to do?" Paris asks.

I don't answer.

"Come on, Zeus. You know what happens if you go against Mason. You remember Tommy Simms."

Yeah, I remember Crackerhead Simms. I remember how he didn't get that nickname until after Mason caught him. This is different.

"I can see those gears turning, Zeusy. I can. And let me tell you what—" he starts.

I punch him dead center of his face with the gun.

"OW! Fuck! Fuck you, Zeus!" he says, holding both hands over his face. I grab him by the elbow and walk him into the bathroom. Still holding on, I force him over into the tub. Blood doesn't come all the way out of upholstery. I've learned that. There might be some cutesy little housewife way to do it in a cookbook somewhere, but I don't know it.

He's still cursing me. Dubois is wide eyed.

The phone rings.

Paris goes quiet for a minute. He knows the rules. No one gets the phone number.

"If you move from this spot, I kill you slow. Do you understand me?" I say. It's not a question.

Paris nods his head as I walk out of the room. I pick up the phone.

"Zeus?" It's her.

"Where is he?" I ask.

"We need to find a meeting place—"

I'm not about to let her run the show, "Where is he?"

"He's safe." They always say that. The implication is that he will remain so as long as I cooperate. The truth is that they couldn't find any other way to manipulate me.

"He had better stay that way, do you understand me?" I ask.

"That's entirely up to you." That line is pretty standard. It's almost like a script.

"Do you have Lincoln Dubois?" She asks.

That makes me pause. She shouldn't know that name. She knows Jimmy whatever-the-hell-we-told-them-his-last-name-was.

There are a couple of different ways to play this. "No, not yet, but I can have him within the hour."

"No need to rush. We will set a time to meet tomorrow."

"What happens to the boy?" I ask.

"Nothing. If you deliver Lincoln Dubois to me unharmed, then nothing at all happens to the boy. You two can go on your sick little way together." That's pretty funny. Her job is to get back a guy that her boss wanted to cut into with power tools while jerking off, but escaped, and she's gonna moralize.

"When?" I ask.

"Noon. Isn't that the time that always works best?"

"Where?" I ask.

"The Aquarium. Near the poisonous fish display."

That professor guy would call this 'Irony'. Capital I.

"Fine."

I hung up the phone doing my best hardass voice. I'm just hoping she's as professional as she's trying to make me believe she is. I look up at Dubois. He's looking at me. That's when I realize. I'm shaking.

33 • The Card

L IVE, DIE, WHAT'S the difference. At some point, everyone goes face up. There's no way to escape that. People try. Jog until they go blue in the face. Even kids. I see kids out jogging all the time. You want to tell them *'go have a hamburger and drink hard whiskey and screw till you can't stand up anymore'*. There's no way to escape it.

Before I worked for Mason, I did my own contracts. Back with Emmaus, he handled the contracts. I was just the stooge. It was pretty sweet. I had my own phone line. My own business card. I never handed it out. I had only made the one. It just said 'Zeus' and then under that 'problems solved' and then the phone number.

This guy called me. Said he wanted someone taken care of. He kept hinting like he wanted me to ask why. I don't do that. It's not my business. The next day the money was where I told him to leave it.

I went to the house and watched. He was unloading groceries. Mid-thirties guy. No kids. No pets. No wife. Nice car. One big bag from the pharmacy and not much else. Special trip for the prescriptions, then. Bought a few other things just to pass time. Single, then.

I went to go get something to eat.

There was already another message on the answering machine when I checked it. I didn't pick it up. One at a time. That's the rule. If you do more than one, you get rushed and sloppy. That can mean hospital time. The union, if there is one, wouldn't want me to tell you that. I left it blinking.

Back to the guy's house. I walk right up to the front door and knock. The door opened and I didn't say anything or smile. His eyes got huge. I shook my head from side to side. Virginia was in the workshop, so it was just me and Wolf. I move in, pressing the guy back into his house and I close the door behind me.

A record played somewhere in the house. Old jazz. In the living room.

Few candles lit on the table. Most of the lights off. He has his dinner sitting on a plate. I motion for him to sit down.

I sit down myself, "Eat," I say. I'll let him finish his meal.

He makes a motion like he's going to say something, but I shake my head side to side. I motion toward his plate. He blinks a few times, then puts the napkin back in his lap and picks up his fork. He stops before skewering a piece of meat and looks back at me. He makes a move to talk again. I set Wolf on the table.

"You don't talk. If I ask questions, you answer by shaking your head yes or no. Got it?" I asked. I was a kid, still. What the fuck did I know?

He nodded. Good. Most don't catch on that fast and I have to break a finger. I smile. Something about me smiling makes him smile. He seems to have gone from the shock of seeing me to calm pretty quickly. It's a little unusual.

"Is there anyone else in the house?" I ask.

He shakes his head from side to side.

"Is anyone going to be here anytime soon?" I ask.

He shakes his head from side to side.

"What's that you're eating?" I ask.

He makes a move as if to speak, then stops himself and cocks his head a little to the side. I smile some. The weird part is he grins back.

I see that when he got up, he left his wineglass on the kitchen counter. I get up and walk to the kitchen and find the open bottle. Red. I walk back to the table with it and his glass.

"You're eating chicken," I say, setting the bottle on the table.

He gets this weird look on his face. He hasn't stopped grinning yet.

"You're supposed to have white wine with chicken," I say. I heard that someplace.

He sits back in his chair a little. His head is still cocked some to the side. He actually looks happy. I don't begrudge him that. It makes things go much smoother.

"Yeah, go ahead. Talk. Why not?" I say, sitting down.

"Fuck them," he says. Girly voice.

"What?" I ask.

"Fuck them for thinking that they can tell me what I can and can't drink with my dinner," he says, smiling. His teeth are perfectly straight.

"Who?" I ask.

"Them. The ones that tell you that if you drink white wine with chicken, everything will turn out okay. The ones that tell you that you have to stop for red lights at two-thirty in the morning on a completely deserted road. Nothing turns out okay. They're wrong. So fuck them. I like red wine, so I drink red wine with chicken. Would you care for some?" he asks, starting to stand up.

I motion downward with my flat palm. He slowly sits down. His grin fades some.

"There's just—there's more on the stove if you'd like," he says.

I don't say anything.

"I know why you're here," he says.

I don't say anything.

"I know why you're here and I'm glad," he says. He's eating in this way that you can only describe as 'well mannered'. You could almost time the bites. It's like watching a dance or something.

He sets the fork down. I can tell he's decided something.

"I'm done eating now." He says, "Do you want to fuck me?" he asks.

I can't help but blink. That caught me off-guard. Not much does.

"Excuse me?" I say.

"You heard me. Do you?" I'm so off kilter I let him stand up. With one arm he sweeps everything off of the table onto the floor. I'm on my feet by then, but I can't seem to bring the gun up. He strips off out of his clothes. Thin little girly body. Tanned, smooth, good muscle tone.

I put the gun right next to his head, handle facing away.

In my life, I've never had better sex. He was very angry about something, I could tell. I let him take that out on me. Why not. He wanted me to beat him up a little while we did it. Just a little. This one wasn't like what I was used to. He asked me to do all kinds of different things. It was nothing I hadn't seen before, only usually I was on the other end of them—and hadn't asked for them. All I ever said was 'sure' and then did them. A few times, he kissed the gun.

Then, he was just laying there on the table. I've never seen anyone glow like that before. I thought that was something guys on soap opera's made up. He was curled on his side on top of the table running his finger up and down the gun.

"When I first got here," I say, pulling my clothes back on, "You were trying to say something. What was it?" I ask.

"It's not important now." Is all he says.

I lean down and kiss him once on the lips. He closes his eyes and smiles.

"Thank you. I feel real again," he says, "Do it now."

I pick up Wolf and put two in his head.

When he exhales, he's smiling.

I search the place. Couple of books I wish I'd taken, but I wasn't into that, then. In his bathroom, though, curiosity gets the best of me. I go back downstairs and in the refrigerator there's that big bag he took in. I take it out and open it. Lots of prescription bottles in there. I read a few of the labels and can't make anything out of them.

In his stack of mail, there's a letter open. I take it out of its envelope and read it.

After I'm done I walk back in and look at the body.

His back is to me. I can't see his head from this angle. He looks like he's just naked and sleeping.

I re-read the last line, *'Your father and I can't. I'm sorry, dear, but we can't. We loved you before you told us you were a sinner. And this Michael boy, whoever he is, was right to leave you to marry a nice girl. Maybe you should have done the same. If you had, maybe you wouldn't have AIDS.'*

I walked out of the house. I got back in my car.

Back at the apartment, I sat down. I just sat there for a little while. I didn't think anything. Finally, I got tired of staring at the blinking light. I walked over to it and tapped the button.

A little girly voice came on saying "Um, Mr. Zeus? I want to cancel the contract that I gave you. You can keep the money for your troubles. Thank you."

It hits me pretty hard. The voice on the answering machine is the same voice that called me with the contract in the first place. It's the same guy whose house I just left. He called a contract on himself. He'd cancelled it before I got there.

That's what he'd been trying to tell me, at first.

I pulled my card out of my pocket. He'd left it sitting near the phone. They almost always do. Tomorrow, I'd take it and leave it with some bartender. That's not very standard. Anyone in the Union can tell you that. If there was one.

34 • Farewell to Paris

G ET UP," I say to Paris.
    He stands up. I can tell from the look in his eye, he knows how this is going to end.

"What are you going to do with me, Zeus?" he asks.

For the first time ever I wonder how many kids have asked him that.

For the first time ever I wonder what he tells them.

Then I wonder what he does to them.

Then I wonder what he did to Gan.

I can tell from the look in his eye, he can see that I'm thinking about these things.

"What room are you staying in?" I ask.

He turns his head a bit to the side, "How did you know—?" he's asking.

"People don't just walk in and get on elevators in a place like this. Maybe across the street, but not here," I say.

He looks like he's about to not tell me where he's staying.

From my pocket, I take out the silencer. I screw it in place. I twist it one extra time, just to make sure. Emmaus taught me that.

"Umm—Zeus?" Dubois says

"Not now, Lincoln," I say, "Where?" I ask. My eyes never leave Paris.

"Across the hall," he says. He says it like he's giving up some huge secret.

"Lets go," I say.

"Wait," he says, bringing up his hands a little.

At that motion, I bring up the gun.

He lowers his hands back down. "Wait," he says, quieter.

I don't say anything. The gun is still pointed at him. I motion with it toward the door. He exhales. Dubois is looking back and forth from me to him like this was a tennis match. In a way, he's not far off.

"Zeus, there's something you and I need to talk about first—" Paris starts

"The door," I say.

He turns. He walks to the door. He opens the door. Before he can get it too far I say, "There are two ways we can do this. You know that. If you even twitch, we'll do it the other way." He pauses. He nods. He walks out the door. I follow.

Dubois falls in behind me.

The door to the other side penthouse is still open. It's a mirror to the first. Red where the one I'm in is white, white where the other is red. I wonder why they'd go through the effort. Paris stops in the middle of the living room.

"Close the doors," I tell Dubois. He walks back to my room and shuts the door. He comes back into this room and closes the door. Paris is still standing there, and as soon as the door closes, I see his shoulders jump.

Then there is a sound from the bedroom.

It sounds like someone with a gag in their mouth.

Paris is sweating.

I walk toward the room. Paris says, "Now, Zeus, look—it's my job—"

"Save it," I say. I walk into the bedroom.

With a little bit of light coming in through the window, I can see someone stretched out on the bed. But the angle is odd. Uncomfortable. I turn on a lamp.

I don't gasp. I don't bring my hand up to my mouth. I've seen too much to do that. I look back out the door to where Paris is standing. He knows not to move. I look back down at the bed.

The eyes are enormous. Begging. He's wet the sheets. He's seen the gun.

Emmaus would call what I did next unthinkable. I'd be kicked out of the Union. If there was one. Looking back on it, I think the only problem was the order I did it in.

I set the gun down.

As I reached toward him, he started to breathe faster. He thinks I'm here to continue what Paris was doing.

In order to untie the wrists, I have to untie the ankles from the wrists. Instead I just pull out my knife. When it clicks, he starts making noises. Pleading noises.

I cut the ropes. His legs thud back to the bed. His arms flop down at his sides.

"You'll have pins and needles for a second," I say, pulling the comforter over the top of him.

I reach toward the ball-gag. What I'm feeling right now is nothing. I take the gag out of his mouth. It's sticky and wet. It smells like fear. What I say is, "Don't try to talk. Just curl up in a little ball and get warm." He does this immediately. I can hear him making swallowing sounds.

What I ask him is, "Do you want me to pull the other thing out?"

He nods his head slowly, looking up at me.

Paris is at the bedroom door.

I reach over to get my gun.

"Now, look, Zeus—I was here to take care—"

I put three in his stomach without even blinking.

"Lincoln. Get him into the tub. Now," I say.

Dubois is doing that while I reach in underneath the sheet.

The eyes are on me. The breathing is shallow.

"Relax yourself as much as you can, or it'll hurt," I say. I have to move his legs some. I grab hold of the base of it.

"Big breath in," I say. He breathes in. It's still pretty shallow.

"Big breath out," I say. As soon as he does, I pull. Just like I thought, it's one that's way too big. His whole body convulses. I don't want to talk about the sound. He goes limp. His color is bad, but his breathing gets better pretty fast.

I pull it out from under the covers. It's dirty.

Dubois has Paris all the way into the bathroom. There isn't too much blood on the carpet. I walk out the sliding glass doors and onto the balcony. I throw it off the balcony. Someone 400 feet below is about to get a very nasty surprise. I don't care.

I walk back inside. I lock the sliding glass doors.

My mind is a bit clearer. I can see the mess that Paris has left on the carpet. I'm going to have to call someone.

I walk into the kitchenette. I get a glass. I put ice in it. I let the water run for a second to test its warmth. Once it's room temperature, I fill the glass almost to the top. Then I take out one of the little bottles of bourbon. I pour a little bit in. I swish the ice cubes around as I'm walking back to the bedroom.

There are hollow thumping sounds from the bathroom. Dubois struggling with Paris. Paris flopping around like a mullet. He won't die for at least ten minutes, I think.

I sit down on the bed. The eyes are still wide. They roll around to me.

"Do you believe that I'm not going to hurt you?" I ask.

The head nods as much as it can.

"Keep the cover around yourself as much as you can. Sit up."

He does. Now that I can see him clearly, he's younger than I thought.

I hold out the water.

"I don't have anything to numb you out, but I have this," I hand it to him. He takes it with both hands. As he brings it to his mouth, "Slowly. VERY slowly," I say. He nods his head and sips. His face convulses a bit with the taste. His eyes never leave the glass.

I stand up and walk to the bathroom.

Dubois is standing there looking at Paris in the bathtub.

"Lincoln. Go to the phone. Call the home office. Tell the secretary that Jimmy needs the number to the cleaning lady. Get that number and call it. Tell whoever answers how to get here," I say.

"But—" Dubois starts.

"Now, Lincoln," I say.

He turns and leaves the room.

It's just Paris and me.

His eyes are on his body. He's shivering. He's holding his belly with both hands.

I close the toilet lid. I sit on top of it. His eyes roll over to me.

"What did you do to Ganymede?" I ask.

His eyes squint a bit.

I set the gun down. I take off the jacket.

"Who—?" he starts.

I punch him. You would think that already having been shot three times would negate the pain of being punched. I've found that is not he case. His head thumps on the wall.

"You were in Mexico. There was a boy there. A preacher's son. His name was Ganymede. You took him. What did you do to him?" I asked.

His eyes still look distant. I punch him again. Again, his head thuds off the side of the tiled wall.

"You delivered him to a man in New Mexico. I had to go pick him up from Mexico and drop off Lincoln Dubois. What did you do to him?" I ask.

His eyes are still squinted. I raise my hand to punch him again.

"Okay, wait," he says. His speech is slurred. I've got maybe five minutes.

"Maybe I do remember," he says, "but why should I tell you?"

I punch him again. His head hits the tile wall this time and doesn't bounce back up. He spits out a tooth and more blood. There is a cough in the next room. Drinking it too fast.

"What I always do, man. Look, Zeus, it's my fucking job. I do my job. I get em and I break them in prior to delivery unless the contract says otherwise. You know that."

"What did you do?" I ask again.

"Look, I'm dying here," he says, "what more can you do to me? When will you be satisfied?"

"What did you do to him?" I ask again.

So he tells me. It's almost like a routine for him. Seven days. Nonstop horrible sex that gets worse and worse each day. Combine that with more and more drugs. It's like on the job training.

They do it in the Porno industry. Girl, guy, it doesn't matter. They have a big group of guys, some nice, some not. If you want in, you have to try out. That means you have sex with some old fucker who always wanted to be in porn but couldn't make it. If you make it in, then you go to training. This means that five to twenty guys who you've never met before have sex with you all day long in various ways and combinations.

When Paris drops them off, they are so disoriented and addicted to drugs, it doesn't matter where they are going. They're happy to get there and away from him. I'm guessing from what I saw out there, he was on his second day.

There was no blood, yet.

When Paris is done telling me what he did to Ganymede, he slumps against the wall. His breathing is going shallow. He's right. There's not much I can do to give him more pain. He's about to die.

So I stand up and put my jacket on.

There is only one way that I can make him pay for what he did.

I pick up my gun.

"Don't leave me, Zeus," he says. His head is against the wall, his eyes on his own legs.

I turn for the door.

"Please. Please don't leave me alone," he says

"Oh, god, Zeus. I don't want to be alone when I die," he says.

I turn off the light.

I shut the bathroom door.

35 • Lions

AFTER THE PROFESSOR, I got interested in learning stuff. I started going to the library. One night while I was there, they had this guy come. He was what the FBI calls a Profiler. A guy who tries to study what it is to be crazy. Only, not like a shrink. A Profiler isn't trying to cure anybody. He's looking at the guy across the table from him and seeing two eyes set looking forward.

That's the difference between predators and other animals. Eyes set forward. There are other things. Claws, fangs, poison, whatever. But the main thing they all share, even spiders, are eyes set forward. Gives better vision. Easier to see prey move.

So the guy is telling us about all the guys he's talked to. I don't know any of them. I guess they're famous guys. Guys who got famous from killing people. No one I know who kills people is famous. We try to keep it that way. It's one of the rules.

He starts talking about these guys and he says that they usually look for places they feel comfortable to hunt. He says that the lion isn't going to hunt in a dense jungle. They don't live there. A lion is going to hunt on the open savannah. That's where the lion is from. It grew up there. It knows what to expect. I can understand that.

For about five seconds, he has me convinced I'm in the wrong job.

Because fine, a guy is abused; his mother threatens to cut off his dick because he wet the bed when he was eight. That's going to mess with you. I don't care who you are. But you grow up, you get therapy or whatever, you find some girl to settle down with and have kids or you start banging supermodel guys, whatever. You don't go out and start skinning people while they're still alive.

What I like most about the guy isn't just his sharp ass suit. What I like is that he cusses on stage. I like that because it means he's being real. He's not trying to use psychological terms. He's not trying to pull one over on the audience. He's just telling us how it is. He calls a rapist a rapist bastard and that's that.

But then he says something that catches my ear. He believes in the death penalty. Until that very minute, I swear to you I'd never thought about it. I knew that guys got put to death for killing. Most people do. But when do you really *think* about why or when or how?

He puts it like this: A wolf that's gone rabid, he says, has to be put down. Why? he asks, because you can't reason with it. It's rabid. Maybe before you could have smacked it on the nose with a rolled up newspaper or something and said, don't try to eat that raccoon or whatever. But it's too late. It's gone rabid. It has to be put down.

When he says it, I swear to you, he sounds sorry to have to say it.

That's when it hits me. He admires them. He admires killers and rapists and the rest because he can imagine what they do. He can imagine it easily. But he can't do it. He can't do it. And that's what he hates most. They can. He can't. Not "because of the law" can't, but *can't*. And he hates that.

The very next words out of his mouth are: because after the first time a wolf has tasted blood, it wants it again. It will always want it. Sharks, Lions, Wolves, it's all the same. Once they've tasted blood, there is no going back. They'll always want it.

I got up and walked out.

36 • The Waiting

I SIT DOWN on the bed. His eyes have followed me over the rim of the cup the whole time. The springs make a soft groaning noise.

"You got a name?" I ask.

"Jacob," he says.

"Jacob," I say.

He nods.

"How long now?" I ask.

"I dunno."

"Two days sound about right?" I ask.

He nods.

"Pretty hungry?" I ask.

He nods.

"My name is Zeus. Was someone waiting on you?"

He shakes his head from side to side. No protector or pimp or whatever they are calling them these days. That means the kid is fairly new. "How long have you been out here?" I ask.

He doesn't answer.

Brown hair. Got a little bit of a curl at the nape. Big green eyes. Bushy eyebrows for a guy this young. Not very heavy. Maybe 100 pounds.

He sips from the glass, which is mostly gone.

"You got clothes around here?" I ask.

He shrugs.

"You feel drugged?" I ask.

"I dunno. Maybe before, but it wore off after—" He trails off. I don't need him to finish.

When Mason made the call, Paris didn't have to go far. I'm thinking that he was interrupted by Mason calling. I'm thinking that must've been what I saw through the doorway when I arrived back here with Dubois.

I stand up and go to the suitcase. I pick it up and put it on the little dresser. I open it. Inside are Paris's clothes. They won't fit right, but right now what's important is that the kid puts on clothes and feels safe. I choose a pair of jeans and a t-shirt and a thick sweatshirt. I toss them all on the bed.

He stares at them. Then back at me.

"We'll get you something to eat and a shower and you can sleep a bit, then we'll talk some. Try to get you back where you belong."

He just stares at me.

I walk to the bedroom door. I grab the handle. I look at him one more time.

"Don't go in the bathroom. Come out when you're dressed," I say. It maybe comes out more harsh than I mean it to. I think he'll be okay.

I close the bedroom door and walk over to the kitchen. Dubois is standing next to the phone.

"Did you call?" I ask.

He nods. He hands me a piece of paper.

The number on it looks kind of familiar. It always does to me. Like I should know it.

By now, Hollywood has let everyone in on one part of the business. That's the Cleaner. It's a terrible job. I wouldn't want to do it. But they make more money than I do with much less danger. Unless you count maybe spilling something on themselves or whatever.

Mason uses a woman. Says it's the only way he can trust the job'll get done right the first time. She's old. She was trained by her husband, who used to work for someone. Someone big on the Italian end of things. One of those names. We all just call her The Cleaning Lady. I pick up the phone. It rings for a second. Then it picks up. In the background I can hear the sounds of kids playing. It sounds outdoors. It sounds like people are singing 'happy birthday'.

"Yes," she says.

"It's Zeus."

"Ah, Zeus. How are you, dear?" She asks.

"Not good. I've made a real mess. I was wondering if you could help me out with it," I say.

"Certainly, dear," she says, all TV grandma sweet.

"Where?" She asks.

I tell her

"About how long ago did the spill happen, dear?" She asks. I can hear her scratching as the pencil moves across the little pad she keeps near the phone. There's probably a reminder on there to pick up the birthday cake for today, too. The ultimate end of Jimmy Paris happens on the same sheet of paper as a reminder to pick up milk. I can't help but smile.

"About five minutes," I say.

"Big mess?" She asks.

"Very," I say.

"Alright, dear," she says, "I'll take care of it today. I suppose your uncle will take care of things, as well?" She asks.

"Yes. He'll do that," I say. Why not charge it to Mason? Let him deal with it. One more thing to get under his skin. Ruin his reputation.

I hang up. Dubois is still pale. He's shaking a little.

The bedroom door opens and Jacob comes out. The clothes hang off of him. He has to hold the pants up. I grab the 'do not disturb' sign off the counter and open the door. I put it on the knob and wait. Dubois files past. Jacob hesitates for a second, then walks past me.

He never once looks back at the bedroom door.

I close Jimmy's door. I take the room key I swiped and slide it under the welcome mat for the cleaning lady to find. Standard procedure. We all walk across the hall to the other room.

Just inside I walk to the bathroom. I start the water running. I check to make sure it's not too hot. When I come out, Jacob is standing at the threshold to the bedroom door.

"I won't tell you everything is going to be alright," I say, "because I dunno if it is. But I'm not going to do anything to you. Get a shower. When you get done, food will be here and you can eat. After that, we'll figure something out."

He just sort of stands there.

I want to pretend I don't know what to do. I want to pretend to be a big man and just walk away. But I know what he needs.

I walk to him. He looks up at me. His eyes seem dead.

"Do you know what a proverb is?" I ask.

He nods his head once.

"There's one that says as soon as you step out your front door, the longest and hardest part of your journey is already done." His eyes fall back down to the floor.

"There's a straight-razor in my bag on the sink," I say, "I know it won't be the first time you've thought about it. You can do it. I won't stop you. But think about this; if you do that, he wins."

He looks back up at me.

"He was trying to break you. To hurt you so bad you wouldn't care what happened to you."

He looks a little to my left.

"So if you do that, he wins," I say.

I walk over to where Dubois is standing. I hear the bedroom door close. My knuckles are white.

"Holy shit, Zeus," Dubois says.

"What?" I ask, not looking at him.

"You—I mean—you're actually a—"

"Shut the fuck up," I say.

Just shut the fuck up.

I order room service. I sit down on the couch. Dubois sits down on the other one.

"You don't have to say 'sorry' or anything, I mean, I know—" he starts.

"Sorry for what?" I ask.

He pauses for a minute, "Well, sorry for—for you know—"

I just look at him. In the background I can hear the shower still running.

"How did you get away?" I ask.

He shudders, "I don't want to talk about it," he says.

"How?" I ask.

He waits a minute, then says, "He took a break. He took a break to go put on some special clothes or something. I was in so much pain from the things he did, but I knew I could still make it, if I could just get away."

I wait.

"He'd left a scalpel on the table. I distracted one of the big guys by— well—I distracted him. While he wasn't paying attention, I picked up the scalpel and brought it up to his—well—his—you know."

I wait.

"So he got me free before his boss came back."

"What about that other guy, the other big one?" I ask.

"He was all blissed out on something. Lights were on, no one was home."

I nod.

Back in the bedroom, the shower stops.

Do I believe that's how it happened? Does it matter?

The knock at the door makes Dubois jump. I walk to it and look through the keyhole. I open it and wheel the cart inside. I tip the guy.

I close the door and lock it.

Just as Jacob comes out of the bathroom. He's got the clothes from the other room on. His hair is all wet and falls in his eyes.

"I didn't know what else to get," I say. I ordered a hamburger and fries. I figured it was a sure thing.

He sits down on the couch. I wheel the cart over to him. He doesn't touch it. He just looks up at me with his hands in his lap.

"I didn't have to help you at all if I was just going to do that," I say.

It seems to be enough for him. He attacks the food.

"Slow down, you'll make yourself sick if you haven't eaten in awhile," I say.

He's got half of the burger done before I finish saying that.

Dubois is smiling. I don't know what about.

I sit down on the couch. For a minute, it's just us watching the boy eat. He doesn't notice. The burger is gone and he's shoveling in fries by the threes. Right next to the glass is a bottle of pain relievers. I'm gonna dose him up after he's done. When he finishes the food, he chugs the soda. When that's gone he just sits there, eyes on the empty plate.

Then he burps.

Dubois laughs. I smile. The kid looks up at us and can't help but grin at the corner of his mouth. "Excuse me," he says.

"I'd order more, but you couldn't eat it. When you wake up," I say. I pick up the bottle of pills. I shake out three. I close the top.

"Here," I say, "take these and go lay down. I'll get more food for you when you wake up." He looks at my hand, then back at me. Then he takes them and puts them in his mouth.

"You can have more of those when you wake up, too." He just sits there for a moment.

I stand up and walk back toward my bedroom. I can hear him follow after a second. I pull back the cover a little. It's still all messed up from Gan. I do not see Gan lying there as he was when I left him this morning. All I see is an empty bed. I try to make myself believe that.

He sits down on the bed. Then he lays back. I put the cover over him. I tuck it up under him in some places. I remember one of the ladies I lived with used to do that. I remember I liked it. He breathes in one big time. Then out one big time.

"Is he your boyfriend?" Jacob asks.

"Dubois? No. Just a guy," I say.

He nods.

I start to get up.

"Stay," he says, then, "please."

I sit back down.

"How long now?" I ask.

"Couple months. Just till I can find a real job," he says.

"You're not old enough to work," I say.

He doesn't say anything.

"No one's helping you?" I ask.

"There was a guy, but he wanted me to start doing needles with people, and other stuff."

I have a pretty good idea what the 'other stuff' is.

"Can you go home?" I ask.

He doesn't say anything.

"Why?" I ask.

"My dad's a preacher. My mom thinks he's some sort of prophet. I watch TV. He's not what you call a 'time-out' kind of father. He likes hammers and knives better." He yawns big, snuggles into the pillow. He was going to say more, I can tell. He's out cold, though. I wait for a minute. Then I tuck more of the sheet in around him.

I stand up and walk back into the living room.

I leave the bedroom door open.

Now, it's just the waiting.

37 • Pictures

EVEN WHEN I was little, I remember people staring at me. I remember that all I really wanted was for them to stop. Women did. Men did. Older boys did. Older girls did. Little girls my own age would sneer that sneer they do.

I didn't understand until later.

I had been staying with a family for a little while. Nothing bad had really happened yet. Not to my body, anyway. I was out walking along the beach. Up under one of those boardwalks. I shouldn't have been alone being that young. I shouldn't have been in that kind of place.

I remember seeing a piece of white plastic sticking out of the sand. I went over to it and pulled. It came free of the wet sand pretty easy. I wiped it against my trunks and then held it up where I could see it. Then, I almost dropped it.

It was a Polaroid.

There was a boy and a man in it.

Only, the man's head was cut off by the top of the picture.

You could see the boys head, though.

You could see that just fine.

I sat down. I remember being dizzy. I remember feeling very small. I remember I couldn't catch my breath.

I heard the lady who had told me to call her mom start calling for me. She was back down the beach. I didn't want to go. I didn't want to move. I felt very small and heavy.

I remember most looking at the thick hair on his belly. How some of it brushed against the boy's smooth cheek. I remember thinking how the boy must have been hurting having his jaw open that wide. His eyes squeezed shut. I remember feeling very small and heavy and weak.

I started crying. So what? I was a little kid. I cried. I felt very small and heavy and weak and hot. I remembered thinking of the men that had told me to call them dad. I remember thinking about how they had thick hair like that. How they had mowed the lawn with thick fur covering their bellies like that.

I wondered if I would have hair covering my belly like that.

The woman who told me to call her mom that year came walking up. I had put the picture under my butt. I just sat there.

"Jeremy?" She had said, walking up to me. That was what they called me back then. She was one of the few that had bothered to learn that name.

"Yeah?" I asked, looking up. She must've seen more than just me crying. She got very white.

"What's the matter?" She said and leaned down to hug me.

I wiggled her hands from around my shoulders. I didn't want anyone touching me. I felt thick. Heavy. Small.

"Will you come back down the beach and sit with your father and I?" She asked.

"In a minute," I said. I couldn't look at her anymore. The water was crashing against the pylons way out at the end of the pier.

She stood up. "Okay," was all she said.

When I did go back down the beach, I wouldn't go near him.

I went back to the hotel room that night still feeling all those things. When she said that it was bath time, I told her I'd bathe myself. She argued some, but not much. I got up on the suitcase and stared at myself in the mirror. I looked a little like the boy in the photograph. Nothing like that man.

I scrubbed so hard that night that I drew blood in places.

The shrink they took me to the next week told them something that made them change how they acted around me. All of a sudden things were just quieter. Softer. There was less hugging. They kept asking how many times I had washed my hands that day. I wondered if they wanted me to do it more often. So I did. When it got up to about two or three times an hour, they told me that the next day, someone would be by to help me pack my things and take me to live with a new family that was very excited about having me there.

The lady who told me to call her mom told me she would still call me all the time and write and that we'd still play checkers together.

I never saw her again. I can't even really remember her face.

But I've never forgotten that man's hands, or the curve of his belly underneath that boy's chin. How wide the boy's mouth was open. How many

wrinkles were in his eyes as they were squeezed shut so tight.
    Never.

38 • Counting the Cost

ON THE WAY from the bedroom, I stop at the table. I pour a drink. I walk over to the couch. I take my jacket off. Virginia and Wolf both staring at Lincoln. I shrug out of the harness and set the guns down on top of the jacket. I sit down next to them. I rub my eyes with my fingers. I look at Dubois.

The ice in the drink clinks against the glass.

"So," says Dubois.

I just let my eyes go out of focus and stare at the little table between us. My eyes go to the bedroom door. Then back.

"So, what happens now?" Dubois asks.

Good question. I don't answer. I don't look at him.

"Zeus," he says.

I look up at him. Then back down.

He crosses his leg. I see for the first time that he's wearing clothes he obviously stole. Even when he had money, these would have been beyond his means.

"Where did you get the clothes from?" I ask.

He looks down at them.

"I took them."

"From who?"

"A guy who gave me a ride."

I nod. I look back down at the floor.

"What happens now?" he asks again.

"We wait," I say.

"For what?"

"Noon."

"What happens at noon?" he asks.

"That's when I deliver you to them and get the boy back," I say.

He goes quiet. I figured he would.

"I don't want to go."

I don't answer.

"What's to stop me from running for the door right now?" he asks.

I look up at him. I see his eyes.

"You won't."

"How do you know?"

"Because there's a chance that if you go, you'll go free. That you won't have to die," I say.

"What if I decide that I know you won't let me go?"

I look up at him. Then I take a sip. It burns my mouth. My eyes close for a second. I open them again. He hasn't moved.

"If you go for the door, you know I shoot you. If you stay put and go tomorrow, you know that maybe I won't be able to get you out, but I'll shoot you to make sure you don't have to go through what he has planned," I say.

He's just looking at me.

"But, there is the chance that I can get you out. Even if it's a slim chance, you're willing to take it," I say.

I sip.

He watches.

"Guys like you don't have what it takes to die. You'd rather wait to see if maybe you can live," I say.

I sip. I set the glass down on the table next to the couch.

"What happens to the boy in there?" he asks.

I grin. Like a shark. "You want a crack at him, Lincoln?" I ask.

He swallows hard, "No."

I stare into his eyes.

"No," he repeats. He looks down. Away.

"After he's slept, I get him more food. Then I tell him where the shelter is. Then, after he leaves, I follow to make sure he goes."

"What if he doesn't?" Dubois asks.

"Some do. Some don't. This one will."

"How do you know?"

The image of him in the other bedroom flashes into my head. Then the image of it being Gan trussed up like that. I feel like putting another bullet in Paris.

"Kids like him don't like what they do. They do it. But they don't want to. Someone just has to show him how to get help to go the other way."

Dubois laughs some, quiet.

"What's funny?" I ask.

"Nothing," he says.

"Tell me," I say.

"It's nothing," he says.

I stare at him.

"Just you."

I stare at him.

"Just you, man. The invincible Zeus, who stops long enough to save kittens and hookers," he says.

I don't say anything. I take another drink. My legs start to feel warm. I feel my shoulders unwind a bit. It's not much of a change. To me, it feels like being naked.

"You going to try to kill Mason?" he asks.

I don't answer.

He shakes his head from side to side, "Shit," he says, "Wasn't there a guy who tried to do that once?"

Yeah. There was. I don't tell him about that, though. I know where that guy is at. Mason left him alive so he'd always know what he'd done. So he'd have to live in the body they left him with after. That won't be me.

"Is this about that gook boy?" he asks.

"Shut the fuck up, Lincoln," I whisper.

"It is. It is, isn't it?" he says.

I stare at him. He's grinning.

"The ass must be real good for you to—"

I move my hand onto the handle of my gun.

He stops talking. His eyes are riveted to the gun.

"Is he worth it?" Dubois asks.

I don't answer.

39 • The Exact Opposite

WRITERS ARE BASTARDS. I've read books. I don't tell people. But I've read books. What has it taught me? I don't know anything about how to criticize a book. I like them or I don't like them. Whatever. But the reason I call them bastards is because they torture people. Maybe not real people. But they torture people.

Especially little boys.

In every book, some little boy is giving some guy a handjob for a soda in the movie theater. In every book, some guy is remembering just what it tasted like when his dad took him on long drives.

It's subtle, too. Even something as simple as a comic book. Take that guy who dresses up in a costume to beat the hell out of bad guys at night because his parents were shot down in front of him. Who thinks up having a little boy watch his parents get gunned down? Who thinks up having him live to tell about it? Later on, that same man watches another boy who's parents die in an accident. He takes that boy in with him. They eventually start fighting crime together. This is a book that kids read.

I guess most shrinks would say "It's a case of Projection." As if that means anything.

There's a guy who writes horror books. He's really good, too. But in a lot of his books, there's some little boy who gets tortured. The kid usually winds up alright, though. That's the difference in his books and everyone else's. He hurts the kid, but the kid winds up okay. The kid winds up stronger, in the end. Shrinks would say "His work shows the resilience of the human psyche at early ages."

What I think is that most people don't see that. Most people see the monster in the movie, but not the little boy.

I do.

I see that every time a guy writes a book, there's some little boy in it who gets tortured or hurt. I see that every time some woman writes a book, the woman in the book is whole and powerful, or becomes that way. What I see is that every time a man writes a book, a little boy winds up dead. Or worse, alive.

I think it's because there isn't anything more beautiful than a child. There. I said it. I'm a man, and I'm not supposed to say shit like that. But there it is. Kids are amazing.

Not like adults.

Teenagers are amazing, too. But for completely separate reasons.

It's like kids are somehow this piece of the Big Bang that gets broken off and put into this tiny frame. I dunno. I'm just talking. I think it's because they are still able to feel and touch and sleep and color with crayons. They haven't become dead men, yet. They are still growing.

To me, little boys are better.

I don't mean sex.

I don't think anyone should ever have sex with kids.

I've met guys who think that it's okay. Dubois, Mason, whatever. They say that kids are sexual and it's okay. That it's just society that says it's wrong.

But I knew those things long before I knew what a law was.

I knew it in my bones the minute I saw that photograph under that pier.

You're supposed to leave them alone. They're supposed to have time to explore their own skin. What guys like Paris do is rob them of time. They take away time.

Because a boy may jerk off six times a day. He may have a habit of lifting up the bottom of his shirt with his thumb to feel the flatness of his stomach with his palm in public. He may notice you watching. He may do things to make sure you keep watching.

But he's not flirting.

That's where guys like Paris get it wrong.

That boy may want your attention. He may even want your attention on his body. But the last thing he wants is you inside him. The last thing he wants is for some guy to get sweat all over his clean skin. What happens when a man has sex with a boy is that he takes away that boy's time to live in his skin. Guys like Paris will tell you I'm wrong. But I see. I've been there.

At some point I guess I'm going to have to talk about what got me started hustling when I left that last foster home. I don't want to. I'll talk about Emmaus. I'll talk about the picture. God, I don't want to talk about that, though.

I guess that means I'm going to have to.

No, I don't mean sex. What I mean is that little boys are still free to feel and sing and dance and color with crayons. They can still be tucked in at night and get cuddled. Even men who want to be with other men lose this. A man trying to cuddle another man is funny to watch. But a little boy fits right into your arms.

It makes me wonder if most guys who write books are trying to show that. Maybe they are just trying to make it clear by showing the exact opposite.

40 • Wade In the Water, Children

I REMEMBER WE made the trip all the way to San Diego. This big water park there. I was just a little older than the whole photograph thing I was astounded. I'd never seen that much water before. That many fish all in one place.

The moment I remember most was standing in front of this enormous tank full of all that water. It was so gigantic, and yet so peaceful. My little hands pressed against the glass. Sharks swimming right next to fish that they would eat if they weren't so well fed. I just wanted to climb into that peace and swim. Just swim for the rest of my life.

"Look, honey, that one is called a lemon shark." A man standing not too far from me was kneeling down near a boy almost as tall as me. The boy, wide-eyed, safe. Loved. I watched them out of the corner of my eye for what seemed like hours. The kid was an endless fountain of questions which his father answered with no anger, no frustration. I wanted to walk up to them. I wanted to ask him to be my father.

I just wanted to swim there.

That's when the guy grabbed my shoulder and forced me along with him to the nearest bathroom. One of the ones that told me to call him 'dad'. It was the worst beating I ever got. The taste of the pencil between my teeth. I had to stay quiet because it was a public place. I remember how mad he got that he 'couldn't get a good god damn swing' in the small stalls.

I had wandered off. I did that a lot when I was a kid. I used to pray that I would get lost and not have to go back. I was still young enough to think someone was listening. That, somehow, the police would find me and see what he'd done. Then they'd come to the house and kill him. When you're a kid, you think like that: that killing the bad guy solves everything. Walt Disney did that to us.

The whole time I stood there, pants around my ankles, snot and tears streaming down my face, I thought about swimming. I almost didn't even feel the belt. I almost didn't hear his heavy breathing, or how cold my legs were getting. There was just me. And swimming.

There's always a part of that memory, though, that I can't get beyond. The beating stopped, I think, and I remember him hissing 'stay quiet'. Then there was a hand on my hip. I don't remember anything else until what must have been about a week later.

Swimming at the local public pool. I was always there early, so I was kind of alone. Not many people. I remember holding my breath and sinking. All the way to the bottom. I just sat there, slowly blowing bubbles up. There was a peace and quiet. I sat there until I was burning inside, like my lungs were about to explode.

They hauled me up. I gasped and sputtered. Pushed the lifeguard away when he tried to give me mouth to mouth. I left, hurried, embarrassed. Ashamed. Everyone thought I had tried to commit suicide.

I was just trying to be alive.

That was one of the early places. It got a lot worse. I think that was the second family I ever stayed with. I don't remember a lot about it. Just that day. Just that feeling. Swimming. Sinking.

Peace.

41 • Not Thinking

IN THE MILITARY a bullet becomes a 'round'. A clip becomes a 'magazine'.

To the cops, a person is a victim. To a guy who does what I do, they get called a lot of things. The movies make it seem like we have a common language. Like all people who get taken out are called a 'mark'. If there was a union, I'm pretty sure they'd want something like that.

The professor told me that's called jargon. It's a collection of words used to make you think they know more than you. They tell you in school that it's learning to be precise with language. You don't talk about the way a guy writes a book, the professor said to me, you talk about his 'rhetoric'. You talk about what 'tropes' he uses.

In math, you don't talk about a number. You talk about an 'integer'.

It's a mask. It's a guy dancing around singing and shaking a rattle. Knowing what is really curing the kid on the blanket is his own body. Knowing that it just needs time and warmth. But if anyone else knows that. If anyone else doesn't see the show he's putting on, he's out of a job.

The higher someone's education in something, the more special words they learn to make sure you feel they know more than you. Forty-five grand buys you a piece of paper and the right to use the word 'discourse'.

'Exploratory surgery' is the doctor's way of saying 'we have no idea what's wrong and we're just guessing at this point' without panicking the family.

I'm thinking all this instead of paying attention to Dubois. He's talking about how he got away. He's talking about what he had to do to get to the city. I'm not listening. I'm not interrupting, either. I need him calm. I need him easy to handle.

One of the things you learn to do when you do what I do is handle people. There are times when you want them begging. When you want them to piss themselves. There are times stuff like that is actually part of the contract.

Someone wants someone else to be utterly humiliated and dead. I've never really understood it, but it's not my thing to go asking a lot of questions.

Especially not to someone who agrees to my price.

If there was a common language for all of us who do this, I'd be called whatever the word is for someone who's very expensive, but worth it. When someone says BMW, it's the same. When someone says Ferrari, it's the same.

I'm a name brand.

I'm thinking about pulling apart Virginia and Wolf. I get a towel from the kitchen and I start doing that while Dubois is talking. When I'm stripping down my guns to clean them, there is no other thought in my head.

Buddhists in Japan would call this Zazen.

I leave one loaded and fully put together while stripping the other.

Dubois is docile right now. I want him that way.

The only thought in my head is the gun. This part connects to this part. This is how to remove this part. This is how this part is cleaned.

I'm not thinking about Gan.

I'm not thinking about how they might be torturing him for fun.

I'm not thinking about how he's laying there wishing I was there to help.

I'm not thinking he needs me.

I'm not.

I'm not thinking.

I'm done with Virginia before I realize it. She's already back together and loaded. As I slide the clip in and get a bullet into the chamber, Dubois shuts up. I look up at him. Then I put Wolf in front of me and break it down.

I'm not thinking about the boy in the bed.

I'm not thinking about how tired I am of there being street kids to save.

I'm not thinking about how I have to do this alone.

I'm not thinking about how you have to have a license to have a gun, and I'm not thinking about how anyone can have a kid.

I'm not thinking about how fucked up that is.

I'm not thinking about how it's killing someone either way.

I'm not thinking.

I'm not.

Wolf is done and I look up. Dubois is asleep. I put a bullet in the chamber and set them down. The towel is dark black with the dirt. I've gotten sloppy. Emmaus would have done really bad things to me if he'd seen how dirty I'd let my guns get.

Fuck him. I've been busy.

The guns go back in the belt. The hands on my watch are around toward nine and six. It's late, but not too late. Now that he's caught, I guess Dubois can finally relax enough to really sleep. I stand up and put my shoulder harness back on. I ease the guns in the holsters. I walk to the bedroom door and move it open a bit.

The boy is still sleeping.

I'm not thinking about his slim waist above the covers and the way his back makes a deep valley for his spine.

I'm not thinking about how much it reminds me of the first time I watched Gan sleep.

I fix another drink for myself. The ice clinks against the sides of the glass.

If there was a main language, most people who use guns would call that sound 'prayer bells'.

What's inside the glass would be 'medicine'.

'Liquid Zen'.

42 • Armor

THE PART OF me that watches me is telling me I haven't slept. I haven't slept in a while. It's telling me that I'm tired. I don't know that I believe that.

What I'm thinking about is how there aren't any women in my life.

What I'm thinking about is that male and female are defined by whether or not one can accept a part of the other inside itself. I'm thinking about how power is defined by the inability to accept something inside. Maybe that's not the right way to say that, though. Maybe it's the unwillingness. At least, that's what they tell me. TV, movies, songs, whatever.

But tell that to the boy sleeping in the bed. Taking things inside him. For money. Choosing to take things into himself for money that keeps him alive. Tell him he has no power.

What I'm thinking is that giving up power actually equates to having an almost infinite supply. A man once told a prisoner 'Today, I come to kill you.' The prisoner replied 'And I choose to let you."

I know. I've been there.

I'm thinking about all the things I've taken inside. Cocks, fingers, blades, bullets. Words. I'm thinking how choosing to let that happen made me.

The part of me that watches me is telling me I haven't slept. I haven't slept in a long time. It's telling me I've closed my eyes, but that means nothing.

I'm thinking how having to take something into yourself that you aren't willing to allow in is the real lack of power. Men like Mason and Paris, this is what they thrive on. Taking someone's power.

I know. I've been there.

This is why little boys are the goal. This is why Mason is a rich man. This is why Paris is dead. Women are trained from birth to have their power. Boys have no way of knowing. No way of defending themselves. The second they get penetrated, the damage is already done. Bullets, blades, cocks, fingers, whatever. Words do way more damage, though. Way more.

Dubois snoring. I'm watching him sleep.

He's one of them, too. Only he doesn't want them broken. He wants them willing. He wants them to moan and wiggle. It's part of his fantasy. Guys like him marry women who have little boys. Guys like him wind up coaches of little league baseball teams. Guys like him wind up priests.

So women have the power. And men know it. So they take it from them with rape. And they take it from little boys with rape. Or bullets. Or words.

And I'm thinking about how books get banned. Books get taken off shelves for getting too close to the truth of something. Guns you have to wait a few days for, but you get them. Books get burned. I'm thinking about what that means.

I'm at the bedroom door before I realize it. I'm watching the boy sleep. I'm trying not to think about watching Gan.

The part of me that watches me reminds me that it's right. I haven't slept. I'm tired. I walk over to the bed. I sit down slowly. The springs groan. I wait a second. Then I take my boots off. I take the gunbelt off. I slide them out of their holsters. I put them both under the pillow. The boy is on the right side of the bed. His back is to me. I lay down on my side. I can see the door. I can feel the boy breathe against my back. I tell the part of me that watches me to count thirty minutes off, then wake me up. I can hear it whispering to itself. It sounds like a kid covering his eyes standing up against a light post just before yelling 'ready or not, here I come'.

I sink under.

White light There is so much white light.

It's burning my eyes. I can't take too much more of it.

My throat is constricted tight. I can't breathe. There is something on top of me. Then it's all clear. Then there is a man in front of me wearing armor. Gleaming armor. A million suns burning in the shine of his armor.

I raise my arm up and there is a gun.

I stare as I pull the trigger.

His armor shatters.

Underneath is a boy. Naked. Shivering. It's me.

Only, when I was very very little.

He reaches out for me. In the shards of the armor there are the two of us reflected. Him in my arms.

Only just holding him is getting him dirty. I'm dripping black oil all over him. He's covered in it. He's choking on it. He can't breathe. He can't breathe.

I can't stop it from going in to his mouth. He can't breathe.

He can't breathe.

I sit bolt upright. Both guns in my hands. Pointed at the bedroom door.

The boy is awake next to me. He's got his feet tucked up under his thighs. He's staring at me.

I breathe in.

Hold.

Breathe out.

Hold.

Breathe in.

I lower the guns.

The boy and I are still alone in the room.

"You okay?" he asks.

I don't answer. I pick up the gunbelt. The part of me that watches me says it's been thirty minutes. I put the guns back in their holsters. I put the gunbelt back over my shoulders and snap it. I put my feet on the floor.

"Are you okay?" The boy asks again.

"Yeah," I say. The boots go on one at a time.

With them on, I stand.

"Where are you going?" he asks.

"How do you feel?" I ask.

"It hurts," he says, "where is he?"

"Dead."

He pauses, then, "I can't pay you back. I don't have anything," he says.

"I didn't ask you to."

"Who was he?"

"Who did he tell you he was?"

"He said something about Houston. I guessed oil or whatever."

I don't say anything.

"Who was he?" he asks.

"He works for a man who sells boys to old men for sex."

"Is that what he was going to do to me?"

"After he was done, it's what would have happened," I answer.

He nods.

"You're going home," I say.

He looks at me, "I can't."

"I'm taking you home."

"They don't want me there."

I walk to his side of the bed. I squat down.

"Do you like it?"

"What do you mean?"

"Not being able to shower off what they smell like at the end of the night."

He looks at me, then away. I don't move.

"Do you like how it feels when there's more than one and you can't get up until they are all done, even the ones that already went going again?"

I can hear his breathing hitch.

"Is that easier?" I ask.

He shakes his head.

"Okay. Then I'm taking you home."

I stand and walk toward the door.

"When?" he asks.

I don't turn around, "I have something to take care of first."

43 • Potato Bug

S EE, THOSE DREAMS are always the same. Bits and pieces. Open elevators with seats, like an amusement ride. One of the books the professor gave me was of poetry. Okay, yeah. I get it. See, poetry is about that. Dreams. On paper. Not like freedom dreams. Like real dreams. The nasty grimy business of what people really think.

There were lots of them in the book. I remember that. I read them all.

Some had stuff to say. Others just seemed to just be a way to fill up a page or two. Those were easy to spot. The ones that were there, though, actually saying something? Those were tough to read.

One woman had lots of poetry in the book. Some woman from New England. She wrote a lot of the stuff. Hid it all away. They didn't find it until after she died. Those were tough to read. All curled in on themselves. The words seemed to be protecting whatever was at the center of those poems.

I thought about it a lot since then.

I think I'm doing that.

I think the guns lead to something else. Otherwise, I would just be some stupid advertisement for cigarettes or something. Maybe I am. Maybe the only important thing is Gan, or kids like him.

Maybe all of us above the age of fifteen are just fucked and need to go away somewhere. Those poems by that woman didn't have me around. Those poems by that woman didn't have to go to school. They curled in on themselves just from being touched by her. They had secrets.

And I've got secrets.

Some secrets I hid so well from myself that I don't even know them. I can feel that. I may not know them, but I can feel that.

So how can any of us do anything right? I kill people to make money. Gan used to have to let men inside his body to make money. I eat because of putting lead in people. Gan ate because he let men leave things in him.

But I didn't.

I don't want him curled around himself anymore.

I want to coax him open.

There's a bug that is all over America. I guess the world, too, but I haven't been anywhere else to see it. It's a little black, segmented ball that opens up into this long, oval thing. Some people call it a Potato Bug. Some call it a Roly-Poly. But they curl around themselves for defense if you pick them up.

After a while, they open back up. If you just sit there, patient, and wait. They open up. Like those poems. Like I hope Gan will.

44 • Books

I REMEMBER THE first night I stayed in a place all my own. It was raining outside. All I had was a blanket, an old mattress and a bookshelf. Someone had thrown them all away.

I was still hurting from the day. This was before Emmaus. I lay down and just looked at the empty bookcase.

One of the only places I ever stayed that was any good was with a martial arts instructor when I was a kid. They took me away from him. But I took him with me in my head. His love of books. We read together. He taught me things from books.

I wanted to put books on that shelf. Even if I hadn't read them. It became a burning desire in me to put books on that shelf. I don't know why. The thought of going out the next day and finding some and then having them and reading them left me warm in the middle.

That night there weren't any, though. And it was cold. So I huddled around myself and went to sleep. In my dreams, there were old rotting hotels filled with books and elevators. Each time I reached to open a book, it fell apart in my hands.

The next day I woke up. I had a few bucks left over. I got some day old doughnuts and went looking. Dumpsters in any city are places to find lots of great things. It was always shocking to me what people would throw away. I went to a few and found some soggy encyclopedias. I lugged those around.

In the next couple I found some old kids books. I thought it would be good to read those. Maybe there would be something in there of what I never had.

It was a fairly large stack that I carried to the next dumpster. That's when they found me. I guess they'd been looking for awhile. I heard the footsteps and turned. There were three of them and a little guy who stood way back at the end of the alley. They were all thick. Two were tall.

"You're that new kid been working around here," One said.

I didn't say anything.

"You didn't ask nobody was it okay you started working here," he said.

I didn't say anything.

They walked toward me and I had nowhere to go. I had no idea what to do.

I dropped the books.

The only thing I remember besides what it sounds like to hear something hit against your own bones, is that it never ended. That once they had me down, and I couldn't hear anymore, I could still feel it. I tried to keep my face out of the large puddle the books had landed in. I didn't want to drown. Not while they were doing what they were doing.

I knew they wouldn't pull my pants back up. I didn't want to be found dead and naked like that.

When they left, I just lay there for a while. Some shrink would probably say I was in shock. It wasn't all that shocking. The beating, what came after. None of this was new. I was just looking at the books.

The water had warped them. Ruined them.

I got up. I pulled my pants back up. I did my best to clean my face off with some of the rainwater that had collected in a can. I walked to the end of the alley and looked to make sure they weren't waiting.

On the way home, I walked slow. I was pretty sure they had broken something in me. It hurt that bad. I didn't feel anything. I didn't think anything. I didn't say anything. In a city like this, that's easy to do. No one wants to see you, anyway.

I just kept walking.

I didn't go back to that place.

The empty bookshelf would be there, and I knew if I ever saw that empty bookshelf I would break down. I'd feel. I couldn't do that. So I just kept walking. Eventually I got to another part of town. I asked around and found out who normally had people working that part. He took me in. Got me cleaned up. Let me heal a while before going back out on the street. That was okay.

It took a while before Emmaus came.

Until the professor, there were no books.

45 • Ruled by Fear

NOT MANY PEOPLE have had to look at a dead body. When they do, it's at a wake or a funeral. Real comfortable. Cozy. Food. Punch. Some woman that they vaguely remember from fourth-of-July barbecues in the corner sobbing loudly.

Most don't have to look at a body they've created. When you shoot someone, you're just as much responsible for that birth as you would be for knocking someone up. That's why the dumb jokes. That's why fourteen-year-old boys tend to make them. They sense, on some level, that this is true.

While I'm asleep, part of me is wondering if Paris is going to get up out of that tub next door and walk over here.

That would make this a very different kind of story.

But I'm still wondering it.

I'm thinking about how most men would be. That's the secret we don't let out. We're all still terrified. We live in a world where all we get told from birth is to separate ourselves from support. A kid who manages to sleep all night in his own bed doesn't get praised for it; he's just being a good boy.

Ask a man sometime if he remembers the first night he slept in a bed all by himself. He was old enough. He could tell you lots of things about that year. But he won't remember this.

It's because he blocks it out.

He has to.

We're told to go master fear on our own without any support.

Girls get cuddled, rocked to sleep. Boys get told to be a man.

It's why we live our lives ruled by our fear.

And desperately try not to show it.

See, horror movies are all based on one idea. That someone walks toward something that they should run away from. There's that old one that I really like. The group of people are just like truckers in space. They haul cargo for a living. The company they work for, though, tells them to go down to this planet and, long story short, they get an alien thing on board. It kills most of the crew except this one woman who refuses to just give up. There were a couple of sequels, I think.

Something in me is thinking that if I wait, Gan will die. That I have to go find him. There is an engine in me, and it's running. Ticking. Just begging to be opened up. I have to find Gan. Only, I can't. I don't know where Leeda would be. I don't even know where to start. I have to be cool and wait for the phone.

Or.

I walk out of the bedroom. Dubois is asleep on the couch. Some guard dog.

I pick up the phone. I bring it to the couch. I grab Dubois by the chin.

"Wake up," I say.

He puts his hand on my wrist. He tries to pull away sleepy clumsy.

"Wake up," I say again.

His eyes open with a start. For a second, I can tell, he saw his monster. He's making sounds instead of speaking.

"I need you to make a phone call."

He rubs his eyes.

"What time is it?"

"It doesn't matter. Late. Pick up the phone."

He stops for a second. He looks at me. Then he picks up the receiver.

"Dial the operator and get the hotel next door."

He dials '0'.

"Yeah, could you patch me through to the hotel next door please?"

He waits for a second.

"Thanks," he looks at me, drops the receiver a little away from his ear, "now what?"

"When they pick up, tell them you were there this afternoon and you left something behind in the room of a woman who is staying there. Ask them if they have anyone with the first name Leeda. Act stupid. Drunk."

His eyebrows come together.

They tell him no. It goes like that for several hotels.

The whole time I'm thinking she's too good to be caught this easy. She'd be under some other name. Maybe I'll get lucky, though. My hope is that she hasn't read any of the rule book that gets handed to everyone who signs up with the union. If there was one.

One hotel does have someone named Leeda staying there. Leeda Swan.

46 • Home

Y OU CAN TURN that up if you want," I say.
The heater is going. The car kind of smells like people. Like lots of people who'd been gathered together in a small space. It's strong smell, but not a bad one.

I look over at Jacob. He's singing along with the song on the radio, only he's just moving his lips. I'm trying not to think about how Ganymede did the same thing.

The freeway is deserted.

He looks at me for a second, then back out the window.

"My dad is never going to let me back in."

"Why's that?"

"He thinks this is against god. That I'm going to Hell or whatever."

I paused for a second. A truck whipped past us. I didn't look at the number on the side of the tank.

"Do you think you are?"

"I don't even believe in Hell," he says.

"What do you believe in?" I ask.

He doesn't say anything for a long time. Then, "If there was a god, why would he have let some of the things that have happened to me happen?"

I don't have an answer for that.

"I'm just a kid, you know?"

I don't have an answer for that, either.

"He's never going to let me in."

There is ice on the road in some places. The frost on the ground is bright white and makes the dirty stalks of dead grass and weeds and wild plants look okay, somehow. We pass people hitchiking from time to time.

"I was doing okay," he says, softer.

"No. You were going to die," I say.

He looks at me.

"Paris would have already seen in you that he couldn't sell you."

His jaw opens some.

"He would have hurt you as bad as he could for his own kicks, then killed you," I say.

When he gets his breath back, he asks, "Why?"

"Cause Jimmy Paris was a sick fuck. Sick."

He nods as if he can understand what I mean. He can't. No one can. No one ever had to clean up after Jimmy but me. I know exactly what he was capable of. Guys like him they don't put in prison; they destroy immediately.

In the animal kingdom, when one member of a pack or grouping of animals goes rabid, the others hunt him down and kill him. This is just the way it is. There are pups or calves or colts or whatever to think about. One goes...off, and the others find him and destroy him. Most won't even eat the meat, no matter how starved. They just leave the outcast's carcass to rot.

"Who is this other boy?" he asks.

"Another boy like you," I answer. Part of me goes paranoid; wants to know how the boy knows.

"Did this Paris guy hurt him?"

"Yes," I answer.

It's quiet. Jacob shuts off the radio. The only sounds are the heater and the wind.

"Do you love him?" he asks.

"It's not right for a grown man to feel like that about a boy."

He waits, "But do you?"

I don't answer.

"It'll be this next exit, up here," he says, pointing.

I turn off onto the ramp and then follow the curve. It's culture shock. The big city is completely gone and now it's just open fields. Gas stations with fast food restaurants attached.

"He's never going to let me in."

"What about your mom?"

"She just does whatever he says."

I wait, then "Why did you leave?"

He looks at me, then back out the window, "They found out some stuff."

"Like what?"

"There's a guy. I dunno. Never mind."

"Like what?" I ask.

He lets out a breath that fogs the window. He starts talking and as he talks, draws geometric shapes in the frost from his breath; "He was a substitute teacher, only Mr. Daniels got so sick he just stayed out. It was a photography class, so there was lots of free time. I dunno. I always really liked it. I guess he kind of saw that."

"Saw what?"

"That I liked the art, that I was excited about it. So he started spending a lot of time with me that he didn't give to the other kids. Most of them were just there to get credit, anyway." He stopped for a moment and admired his work. Crop circles on a rental car window.

"We were in the dark room this one time, and he accidentally touched me and got real embarrassed—only he saw that I didn't mind. I dunno what happened after that, really. It was nice, though. He was always real nice." With his hand, he wiped away the designs.

"It'll be the next street up," he said after a time.

I turned. The road was narrow, and the lawns came right up to the curb. Half-height chain link fences on back yards. Fireplugs not blocked by cars. Some of the houses had Christmas lights up.

I could see he was shaking some. He kept his hands in his jacket pockets. He looked out the side window the whole time.

"Next street."

I turned.

"Third house. That one," he said, pointing.

I pulled into the driveway. There was a dog out back barking at us. Two cars in the garage. The porch light came on. A face appeared at the window.

He sat in the seat not moving.

"Home," I said.

He bit his lip, then reached for the door handle. His hand rested on it for a moment, then he pulled and opened the door. He stepped out of the car. He stood there. The face at the door was still squinting. They couldn't see him yet.

"So do you?" he asked, leaning back down.

"Do I what?"

"Do you love him?"

I looked away. He looked at me for a moment longer, then closed the door. I watched as he walked up to the porch. As soon as he got into the light, the door swung open and a woman in a robe rushed out. She grabbed him into a hug that looked like it might break him.

I put the car in reverse and backed down the driveway. The dog had stopped barking. I turned the nose of the car so that it pointed toward the main street again. Just as I did, one last look back showed a man standing next to the woman. While she had Jacob in a bearhug, the man had his arms around both.

They were so wound up in their circle, they didn't even look at me as I pulled away.

47 • The Boy Who Should Have Saved Me

BEFORE EMMAUS CAME along, I got beat up a lot. In all the books about writing, they say to talk about shit that makes you cringe. So there it is. I was little, and new to the corners. They beat me up.

I took it. When they were hitting and kicking and spitting, I just shut off and took it. Your whole body is just a big pile of meat is what Emmaus would eventually tell me, but I already knew. The shrink called it 'dissociation'. I called it living.

I called it being alive.

Mostly it was just this one guy and his friends, if you could call them that. They were all street kids who worked for a guy named Randall. Couple did stuff for money like me, couple of them were good at breaking in places, couple sold stuff to the upper Park Avenue crowd. Some did all of the above.

The guy's name I forget, but I'll always remember that face. When he first started out, I heard, he was one of the ones who did stuff with old guys for money. One of them got pissed off and cut his face up pretty bad. He had an extremely high pain tolerance, so he got all the weirdo customers. The guy who did it to him had just gotten out from twenty-five to life. Had a little pent-up anger to work off.

He hadn't expected the kid to live.

The upside was that he didn't have to suck cock for money anymore. Randall took care of him and turned him into something like a next-in-command.

I was just off the bus and walking around when I saw him the first time. I wasn't as good at sizing people up back then, so I didn't realize what I was dealing with. I walked right into him because I wasn't paying attention. He and his buddies hauled me into the bathroom. They took me into the handicapped stall, and closed the door. I don't remember too much of what happened after except that I kept trying to stay on my feet.

One of the kids kept watch outside the door. They had a routine all worked out for this. That's what kind of guys they were.

After they were all done, the main guy waited. I was just leaning against the wall and he told me to pull my pants up. When I didn't, he slapped me. For some reason, I don't remember what they did as hurting, but I remember that slap. It stung worse than just about any other pain I've ever had to go through.

I pulled my pants up and he said, dead cold voice, that if he ever saw my face again, he'd kill me.

He and his friends left the bathroom laughing and horsing around with each other.

The boy I should have listened to is the one that found me.

I have no idea how long I was just there, leaning against the wall. He came in and saw me through the half-open stall door. He approached slow and pushed the door open just a bit.

"You okay?" he asked

I didn't answer. He got a look on his face and somehow, he knew.

"Can you still walk?" he asked.

I nodded without looking at him.

He put his arm around my shoulders and under my armpit and I sagged against him. He walked me out of the bathroom. I remember he smelled like something familiar, but I couldn't figure out what it was.

"Do you have a place to stay?" he asked.

I shook my head. Something in his back pocket kept scraping against my ribcage, and I wanted to reach down to see what it was, but I couldn't.

He started walking with me. I could tell he was already tired, but he didn't slow down or let go the whole way down the street. I kept looking to see if they were around. I saw their faces everywhere. Their jagged grins hovered just above my eyes in every face I saw.

Eventually he took me to the shelter. We took care of the little bit of paperwork and he walked me to a bed. He helped me ease myself onto it. Then he sat down on the cot next to mine.

"Are you bleeding?" he asked.

I nodded against the pillow. I had only been in the city an hour or so, and already I was bleeding. I should have taken that as a sign.

From his back pocket he took out a worn out notebook. It was beaten almost beyond recognition. He pulled a pen out of that same pocket and flipped open the book. I could see page upon page of his handwriting. His eyes flickered over the lines, but at the same time, had gone somewhere else. He wasn't totally here.

He started to scratch words onto the page and I went unconscious.

I woke up to darkness. The entire shelter was lights out. All I could see was the light over the desk in the far corner near the door. I felt a blanket on top of me. Someone must have put it there.

The guy was asleep on the cot next to mine. That notebook was underneath the pillow. I lay there for some time thinking how much I wanted to know what he had just written.

Ben was his name. I found that out the next day. A teenage, scrawny junky who would do anything you asked him to for a fix. He was my same age, but because of how he'd been used, he seemed much older.

That next morning he stayed around just long enough to make sure I had breakfast, then said goodbye. I didn't want him to go.

"How the fuck am I gonna survive?" I asked.

He got that look in his eyes again, and pulled out the notebook. He slashed the pen across the page.

"What's that?" I asked.

"My journal," he said.

"What's in it?" I asked.

"My stuff."

He paused. After a second, he put the pen back in his pocket and closed the notebook.

"What stuff?" I asked.

"Stories, poems—stuff," he said.

"Am I in there?"

"Yeah," he said, sipping the last of his orange juice.

"I want to see," I said.

He looked for a second as if he was about to show me, then he shook his head, "No."

"Why not?" I asked.

"Because it's personal. It's personal stuff."

"What do you write about?" I asked. I was ready to talk about anything to make him stay at that table.

"Things that happen."

"To you?"

"To anyone. Ideas, things that happen—it's just a place to put stuff so I'll remember it."

"Are you gonna get some of it published?"

"Someday. Yeah. I want to."

As he spoke, he rubbed his palm against his forearm. It was raw and scabby with old needle marks. I stared.

"Yeah. Someday," he said again, noticing where I was looking.

"Let me read something," I asked.

"No."

"Please?" I asked.

"No."

"Come on," I said.

He paused. Then he said, "Okay. But this means you and me, we're best friends from now on." I didn't know what that meant, but it sounded warm. I liked it. I was like that as a kid.

He opened the book and there I was. What he'd written about me. A couple of pages about how he found me and how I was sleeping. He had that way of putting words together. I can't explain it. It's just that way of doing it where you know someone's good. How I'm telling the story is nothing like he had it written there.

"What's 'The David'?" I asked. He'd said something about the light hitting me from the skylights as I slept.

"It's a statue. You've never seen 'The David'?"

I shook my head.

That next day, he took me to the museum. He talked about art and artists and showed me things. He said that there were a lot of people who knew about art, but very few artists. He was constantly flipping open the book. I asked why and he said that a good writer is always watching people. He said, like the statue, the closer you get to real life, the more like art something is.

For a little while, things were good. That's all I can say about that. He wrote lots in that notebook and showed me all of it. I told him about what things he wrote made me think and he wrote about that. The book was really ratty and beat up and it was about to fall apart, though.

I decided without telling him that the next bit of money I made, I was going to go get him a new one. I couldn't hustle a lot, because I was still hurting, but I went out without him one afternoon and did one. I had to bite my own hand to keep from screaming it hurt so bad, but I got some money.

He cried when I gave him that new notebook. I don't know why it was okay, or what happened, but that night, we slept on the same cot. He put his arm around my ribs, and tucked his hand up under me. In my life, I've never slept as soundly as I did that night.

I didn't find out that he was one of the ones who'd run away from Randall until later. Once a guy like Randall has you, he's got you. You never get away. But Ben had run. Ben was trying to stop. He was trying to get off the needle. We were sitting looking out at the statue in the harbor a few nights later and he told me that his biggest dream was to get something published. He wanted to clean himself up and show up on his mom's doorstep and have her take him back.

Almost a week to the day from when I got him the new notebook, he was dead. Randall's guys just happened to find us. We'd gone with this one guy we both knew who was decent to us. He got what he wanted and then he left us alone to sleep and eat out of his refrigerator and watch his TV We were both just looking forward to getting it done so we could get a shower.

But they were just coming out of a sandwich shop near the guy's apartment. The guy tried to intervene, but they threatened him with a knife. Then they pulled Ben and I around the back, near the dumpsters. They beat me pretty bad. Then they made me watch what they did to Ben.

Then they killed him.

I think after that, they all ganged up on me like they had that first night in the city, but I don't remember. Something inside me went cold and jagged and I don't remember feeling my skin.

They kept finding me and beating me every few days, but eventually they lost interest. Their heart wasn't in it anymore. Most of those next few weeks was a blur until Emmaus. Something about the look in his eyes when they were on me brought a part of me back.

But, even at the time, I knew there was a part that was never coming back again.

48 • Get the Lead Out

I WENT TO WORK for Mason to get away from the people who almost killed me. I met Emmaus because I was one of Mason's boys. I learned to kill people from Emmaus so that I'd never have to let someone inside me again; so that I could put lead inside them. I took Dubois to die because Mason told me to. I met Ganymede because Mason told me to take Dubois to be killed.

I listened to the hum of the heater. Dubois in the next seat, breathing. The tires crunching snow.

I had to rescue Gan, or else he'd wind up like me. Or dead. I had to give Dubois the chance to get away. What this means is that I'm going to have to die. I'm going to have to figure out how to disappear. Completely.

The professor told me about all kinds of rituals. Almost all religions, he'd told me, have a ritual of rebirth. Some thing they do to mark your birth as a new person on their particular spiritual path. They all do it differently though. Think flavors of ice cream. Which religion you feel comfortable with depends on which set of rituals you decide are okay. Which flavor you like best.

"I'm going to have to die," I say outloud.

"What?" Dubois asks.

I don't answer. I know it's the truth. I can feel that.

Paris may not be around, but that won't stop Mason from sending someone else. From getting more boys to sell. Nothing would do that except for him to die. For someone to force him to be reborn somewhere else.

That's the problem with guys like that: You can kill them all you want, but they are reborn and come at you again. The crazies in Texas are right; Hitler is still alive. Only, right now, he's likely some twelve year old guy from the projects who mutilates cats behind dumpsters for kicks. Some people call that 'evil'. I don't know what to call it, but I know it's there.

To just about anybody, Dubois would be evil. I am. I've heard them say it. I guess it's all a matter of perspective. If this were a book, most authors would tell it from Gan's point of view, I guess. They'd make him out to be a tragic figure. A young male tragic figure. Writers like to torture the fuck out of young male tragic figures.

For a second, I think how I'd love to be that author. Then I'd be what the Professor said was 'omniscient'. All seeing. I'd know Gan's thoughts. More, I'd know where he was.

But instead I'm a hitman. I don't even belong to the union, if there is one. Until two weeks ago, I worked for a guy who bought and sold young boys and men on a sex slave market.

There are only three things on my 'to do' list now.
1. get Ganymede back/let Dubois go
2. kill Mason
3. disappear forever.

"You're really quiet," Dubois said. He seems tragic. Maybe he's the main character. Maybe some writer somewhere started this story off with him. Who knows.

After I picked him up from the rest area I dropped him off to take Jacob home, he wanted to talk. About anything. He started talking about everything he'd ever done in his life. How horrible he felt seeing it from the other side. I didn't say anything, but he kept on.

Finally, I lost it: "You have no idea," was all I said. Even I got goosebumps at the ice in my voice.

"About what?" he asked, looking in my direction, but trying to not look in my eyes.

"You don't know what it's like. You have no idea. Stop sitting here thinking you do because you don't. One boy's story? You know nothing."

"What I meant was—"

"I know what you meant. You think because some moderately fucked up shit has happened to you, that you suddenly understand what it's like for them?" I didn't say 'us'.

"That's not what I meant—"

"Then what did you mean? Because that's what you said."

I couldn't believe what I was saying. It was like listening to someone else talk from my mouth. Whining. I was actually whining. Me. To Lincoln.

"I'm sorry," he said.

I didn't say anything. Enough damage. I was remembering things I didn't want to remember, and sounding like a bitch about it.

"We're not better than Paris," I said.

"That's not true—," he started.

"It is. No one wants to think it, so we make up some imaginary line and put him on one side and us on the other. It's all the same, though."

"What? You think age has anything to do with sex?" he said.

"It doesn't seem to on the surface, but it does. It does."

"Your friend Paris was going to kill that boy, right? You said so."

"Yes."

"Did *you* want to kill him?"

I didn't say anything. I'd never been into the violent shit. Never. Not when I was working the street, and not later when I was constantly around the boys. Some of the boys were, and they'd wanted it, but I'd talked them down from it.

"See?" he said, then laughed that little laugh people do when they think they've scored a point on you.

"What," I said.

"Nothing."

"No, what."

"It's just funny, that's all."

"What is."

"You."

"What's funny about me."

"You kill people. You break people's arms. You shoot guys in the stomach and talk to them while they bleed. But you have no idea what's right and what's wrong," he said.

"So?"

"So, I think it's funny. I mean, yeah, I do things that I shouldn't do sometimes, but I don't hurt anyone. You go around like this judge and jury all rolled into one, but you have no idea what's really okay and what isn't."

"You're saying it's okay to do what we do to them?"

"I'm saying that there is a line between guys like you and me and guys like your friend Paris."

"You sound like one of those fuckers from NAMBLA or something."

"No. I'm just saying."

"Just saying what? That it's okay to do what we do?"

"Maybe not okay, but prostitution isn't okay, either. Yet people have been doing it since the beginning of everything. Everyone does it a little."

"What do you mean by that."

"Even when someone's not getting paid for sex, they are still getting something for it. It's a bargaining chip. Come on, Zeus. You have to have seen all this by now."

I had. I guess I had, because it wasn't very shocking.

"I'm not saying that we should get humanitarian of the year for doing what we do, but then I'm not going to say that we should walk into a police station and hold our hands up and say 'take me away', either."

"Don't start with that whole Roman Empire shit."

"I won't. But you already know. This country is all fucked up anyway in how it looks at stuff. We can't help it. We're a country that's come from abusive parents."

I didn't say anything for awhile.

But I felt lighter.

Like all that lead that had been put inside me was lessened somehow. That maybe the score was balancing.

"When I was a kid," he said, "in church, I read this one passage of the bible, and do you know what it told me?"

I didn't say anything.

"Jesus died for all our sins."

I didn't say anything.

"Meaning that all our sins have already been weighed, measured, and catalogued."

I adjusted the heater down a little.

"It's called 'grace'. It's free, and it covers everything. It's kind of like a blank check."

I waited.

"So I went to ask my youth pastor about it. And do you know what he said?"

I waited.

"He said I was wrong. But since then, I've asked lots of people who know a lot more than he did, and you know what they told me?"

I waited.

"That I'm right. That I guessed right. That no one tells anyone that because no one would believe it until they were ready to read it for themselves. Do you know what that means?" he asked.

I could see where he was going with this.

"Because no one, down inside, wants to be okay. They don't want the burden of feeling that they are okay. It would mean that we were already the best that we could be. No one wants to feel the weight of that," he said, then went silent for a time.

The exit came up. I felt lighter. A little, anyway. I didn't know if I'd be strong enough to get Gan away, but there was no going back now.

"So you're saying it's okay to do whatever? To break laws?" I said.

"I'm saying that the guys who make laws put on their pants one leg at a time, too. They have kids who smoke pot when they're not home. They have a wife who eyes the guy in the produce section of the supermarket. They jerk off to pictures of little girls on the internet. Whatever."

For some reason, I was buying into this. I should have killed him a long time ago, but I was listening. And I was changing.

"I wish there was some way for everyone to just come clean about everything so that we could all relax and accept it and maybe sort out some of the guys like your friend Paris from the ones who aren't hurting anybody."

The hotel we were looking for was about two more streets up. I had to work fast. I did the mental picture to get myself ready. I kept thinking how it might be too late, though. I needed to be hard and jagged inside for this. But maybe Dubois had just gotten me killed.

"You're not going to let them have me?" he asked.

"No."

"Either way, right?"

"Either way. Now shut the fuck up," I said.

I hated the sick feeling I got when I started to get heavy again. The lead pouring into my belly. Thinking about men and their smell hovering over me. Thinking about their faces contorting with each thrust. Thinking about the garbage bags that dripped blood. Thinking about all the foster fathers who wanted to get me in the bedroom and then make me go mow the lawn like nothing was wrong.

I had had a few minutes lighter, though.

I didn't know if I could go all the way back.

49 • Approaching Ganymede

NO ONE REALLY cares about any of this. It's all happening too fast for anyone to grasp. The Professor would have called this 'high postmodernism'. He would have pointed out that there were lots of books like what I'm saying. The real problem is that the perspective jumps around too much; at one point it's the past, at some point, it's the future. It's all mixed up and who has time to care about any one person?

Life is like that.

I'm thinking all this as I put the car in park. I'm thinking all this as I look at Dubois. He's thinking something, as he looks at me, but I can't tell what. Minute by minute, I'm losing my ability to do the things I once did. I can't tell what he's going to do or say. He's surprised me. I don't know what that means. I don't know what's about to happen.

I open the door and put one foot on the ground. It feels shaky. If there was a union, there would be a rule against performing any difficult operations or operating heavy machinery if you felt like this.

If there was one, I could get my membership pulled for ignoring that rule.

"What room are they in?" Dubois asks.

"I don't know."

Pause, then "Then how are you going to find them?"

"I don't know."

Pause. I put both feet on the ground. I stand up.

"We could just go back to the hotel and wait for them to call us," he says.

I shake my head.

"Then how are you going to find them?"

"I don't know."

I step all the way out and close the door. I walk around to his side. The footsteps echo and bounce back to me from all sides. Underground parking garage. Modern concrete cave. It's disorienting. Reflected in the window, just in front of his face, is mine. I stop for a second. Something has changed.

He rolls the window down.

"I don't care what you see," I say, "if you see me coming up toward this car and I don't give you this? Do not open the doors," I say, showing him two fingers crossed over each other held up.

"The boy scout salute?" he asks.

I don't say anything.

"Alright."

I turn and walk toward the elevator. The echoes continue. I have to stop myself from looking over my shoulder every few seconds. Up above, the air is whipping past. Down here, it sounds like whistling. It sounds like being chased by someone who whistles.

I press the button and the doors ding politely and slide open. I step inside. They have carpet. The doors slide closed. I close my eyes with them. I stick my finger out and press one of the buttons at random.

The Professor said a guy named Jung thought there was no such thing as coincidences. Something called 'synchronicity'. Before, I didn't know what to think about that. Now? I'm pretty sure he's right.

A small lurch in my stomach. The elevator is moving upward. My eyes are still closed. I pull Virginia from her holster. It feels right. Another lurch, and then a pause. The doors ding and slide open. I open my eyes slow, matching the pace of the doors. I exhale at the same time. Somewhere, in the back of my head, a single syllable is being repeated. It shakes my whole body. I step out onto the floor.

Inhale. Feel the cold air come into me. Exhale. Feel the cold air go out of me. Step. Again. Again. Each exhale takes out some of the black air trapped in my deep spaces. The caves of me. The bad air.

221,219,217. On my right side, the numbers pass slow along. Inhale. 215, 213. How many hotels like this have I been in. How many times have I done this walk. It seems fresh every time. My body is still spring-coil loaded, hair-trigger ready. Exhale. 211,209.

Up ahead. On my left. 206. Inhale. Exhale. Not enough black air out. Not enough loose slack. Pause.

Inhale.

I kick the door in. There's a special way you have to do it to make sure the door doesn't bounce back off the wall and hit you. That looks sloppy. If there was a union, that's one of the things they'd show you. If there was a union.

Glance to the right. The sheets are messed up. I swing into the bathroom with Virginia, eyes flash in, then flash over to the rest of the room. No one in the bathroom. Swing gun toward the rest of the room, close bathroom door. Emmaus taught me that. Check a room, confirm it's empty, close the door. That way, if you missed someone, you'll know if they come out at you later. The noise of the door may not be much warning, but for guys like him it was more than enough time. For me, too.

Into the room. Sheets messed up. Gan's smell. His socks are on the bed nearest the bathroom wall. The other bed is less messed up. Styrofoam cup on the table. Sliding glass door open. Curtains flutter.

I kick over the mattress from one bed onto the other. I've gotten burned like that before. No one under. Nice light thump as one mattress hits the other. No one under them. I move toward the curtain.

You know that sinking feeling that you have just before something is going to happen that will wreck your day? I'm having that. Inhale.

Exhale.

Step through the curtain.

No one on the balcony. Quick step back inside. It doesn't do to have too many people see you on the balcony of a room you're not registered in with a gun. Tends to scare people a bit if they're sunbathing at the pool.

The room is empty. I open the bathroom door again. Empty.

Except for lipstick on the mirror.

How cliche is that.

He's with me and he's safe. Nice try, though. Noon, still. Bring DuBois.

So she knows now. Okay.

I walk back into the room. I close the front door as the elevator doors soft ding down the hallway. I sit down on the bed.

Inhale.

Exhale.

"Shit," I say.

50 • Upon a Time

ONCE UPON A time, there was a man. He worked for his father installing machines in grocery stores. He wasn't happy doing this, but he had no real skill at anything else. He wasn't great at this, either.

In his father's office, there was a woman. She answered phones and filed billing receipts. She was exceptionally good at this.

He didn't date much. She didn't date much. You see where this is going.

About ten months later, she screamed for ten hours and out of her came a little boy. She loved him, even before they cleaned him off. She thought that maybe it was just the drugs, but the next day she still loved him.

She thought maybe it was enough to love her baby boy. Maybe it would help her love the man she married, too. It was a panic thought. Men have them, too. It's a leftover from when we're little and need soothing. We'll believe anything a parent tells us. And they'll tell us anything at four in the morning if it means they can get back to sleep. You get addicted to that.

Five years later, when she caught her husband with one of the neighbors, she thought she'd die. Not from the hurt of love gone wrong, but from embarrassment.

Two years later, the teacher called her at work one afternoon. She sounded shaken. The woman rushed to the school to find out that her little boy, her beautiful little baby, had been hurt badly by some men who had been there to fix a section of roof damaged in a recent storm. No one had known he was missing. No one had found him in time to stop what they'd done to the boy.

The men were found guilty, but because the laws weren't new at the time, they didn't serve much time in prison. They're not important, though, to the rest of the story. The damage they did could have been healed, eventually. Maybe. Given time. And love.

But no one knew how to treat the boy. They were afraid to touch him. He got quiet. His eyes seemed to fix on one place and stay there until someone called his name.

She got another call to the school three years later. Her boy had been accused of doing to another boy what had been done to him by the men. It was dismissed. She thought she'd die of embarrassment.

There was a call to the local skating rink. Her boy was accused of doing to another boy what had been done to him by the men. She was called down to the police station. It was dismissed. She thought she'd die of embarrassment.

They're house was broken into later that year. All that was stolen was a pistol. The thieves were very crafty; no sign of forced locks or broken windows was found.

No more phone calls came.

Three years later, she found her husband making love to her son on the living room couch. It came out at the police station that he'd been having sex with every single babysitter they'd ever had, and all the candy-striper girls at the hospital, and her own son for years now. It turned out that her husband had a voracious appetite for sex. She had had no idea. Her sheets were always cold when she woke up.

The divorce was quiet and quick.

The boy was given to the father because the laws weren't new, then.

The boy ran away. When he came back, they placed him in the Foster Care system. By this time the mother was popping pills just to speak English. And the pistol turned up, finally. The father used it to kill himself.

51 • Self-Defeating Thoughts

THINKING IS A bad idea. Always has been. A Zen Buddhist would look at what's going on and say "You too much think. Too long here," he'd say, and touch my head. That's if he was a nice guy. Most older Dōgen would smack me in the head and say to go sweep the parking lot. The idea is that doing something drives thoughts from your head.

What I wonder is what most people do. What they actually do. I wonder at what point any run of the mill person would fold up his cards, slide his chair back, and walk away from the table. I'm wondering all this while I'm sitting on the edge of the bed, still.

I'm going to have to kill her. Whenever I think her, my chest gets tight. I think about wet softness. Why would a woman get involved in this business? If there was a union, there should be rules against that. Fuck being politically correct. This is not women's work.

Women are too logical to take anything personal.

I hardly notice that I'm already in the elevator on the way down. On the speakers is some horrible muzak version of that song from the 60's. The one with the nonsense lyrics about riders coming on the storm. That song used to give me chills. Here it's just silly. It doesn't fit.

As I open the door, Dubois just looks at me. He doesn't say anything as I start the car and back out of the parking space. He doesn't say anything until we're already on the freeway heading out of the city.

"Well?" he manages.

"They weren't there," I say.

His jaw opens a little, "I can see that. What are we gonna do about it?"

Something in me gives.

I pull the car off onto a ramp leading to a small road. Dubois is holding onto the dashboard. I pull around behind a deserted gas station. I put the car in park, then shut it off. I start to cry.

Dubois has no idea how to react to this. Through the blur, I can tell he's trying to hide his eyes.

I guess if I'd experienced any of what I'm feeling at this point, I'd know what to call them. I don't. Instead it's just this barrage of things. It hurts a lot.

"It's gonna be okay," Dubois says, "You're gonna get him back." He reaches out to touch me.

I grab his wrist and twist it. He yelps. I don't want to do what I'm about to do, but it's all I know. I use the leverage of his arm to pin his face against the window. I lean over and open the door, shoving him out with the levered arm. He goes face down onto the concrete.

I have to do something to drive the thoughts out.

My boot makes a soft whump sound going into his ribs. Again. Again. He can't get enough breath to beg me to stop. I am stomping him. He's fighting to get air.

Something about how he looks makes me feel.

I grab him by the hair and drag him to the back door. I open it and toss him onto the back seat, face down. It's as if there's no sound anymore. I can see him, bloody, moving his lips. He's saying something, but I have no idea what it is.

It only takes a second once I pull his pants down to his ankles. His lips mostly stop moving after a second. He just lays there, taking it. His face dead. I've seen that look before.

It's perfect Zen.

When I'm done, I walk away. I'm standing on the other end of the concrete slab of this abandoned gas station listening to huge eighteen-wheelers fly by. My back is to the car. I'm not thinking anything.

I hear his tennis shoes scrape the concrete behind me.

"Feel better?" he asks.

I don't say anything.

"It's okay, you know. If it helped, I mean."

I don't say anything.

I hear a cigarette lighter. I smell smoke. I hear him exhale.

"It's all anyone's ever wanted from me, anyway. Sometimes I think it's why I was put here."

I don't say anything.

"I guess that's why I did what I did. Although, I was never—like that— not with them—"

I'm trying to read the numbers on the trailers as they fly by.

"It's a big cycle, I guess."

I can't remember what the numbers mean.

"I don't mind, is what I'm saying." Inhale. Cough. Grunt of pain. Sound of tennis shoes scraping gravel.

Stop. "We'd better hurry. If you're gonna find him."

One goes by. I can read the number. Pure Oxygen. I remember that number.

I turn around. I look at him. At what I've done. I look over at the abandoned building. I walk toward one of the doors on the back side where we're standing.

It's locked. I look at him. I pull Wolf and shoot the knob off. I open the door. It's an old bathroom. I step in. Turn the faucet handles. Water comes out. I step back out.

He's just looking at me.

I motion for him to come here.

"You can't kill me. You need me now," he says.

"I'm not going to kill you. Come here," I say.

He walks toward me in small half steps.

I turn on the light. I close the door behind us. The mirror is broken, but he tries to look into it. "Don't," I say.

I pull out the paper towels from the dispenser. I turn to him and reach for his shirt.

"What are you doing?" he asks.

"Shut up," I say. I pull his shirt off. Huge reddish purple marks growing along his ribcage already. I turn on the faucet to get hot water. He's looking at me.

He looks pitiful. His small ribcage. His thin chest. His skin is so light that I can trace veins in some places. But he's standing there, holding one arm up exactly where I left it. I run one paper towel under the scalding water. I press it over the mark on his ribs. He yelps.

"Shut up," I tell him. He bites his lower lip and closes his eyes tight.

For a second, I can see him as a boy. I can see what he must've looked like to that priest. Holding the towel to his ribcage, I run the other hand over his chest and ribs. No jagged points. I didn't hurt him too bad. Not his ribs, at least.

"You're hands are cold," he says, hushed.

I get another paper towel with my free hand and run it under the water.

I wipe just underneath his eyes. He looks at the ceiling.

I let the second towel drop. I can see him as a boy; scared and pitiful.

I kiss him.

It takes him a second to kiss back.

"I'm sorry," I say.

"I know," he says back.

And we were soft together.

52 • Doing Time

I REMEMBER SEEING on the news a while back how this guy used a boy he had sex with. It was down south somewhere. I didn't know the guy. He was too poor to be able to afford anything from Mason. The kid was just some poor white kid he knew.

The kid killed his own father. It's not tough to guess why. The guy must've found out what his neighbor was up to. The kid got off pretty easy because he had a baby face. He talked really polite on the stand, too. That usually helps. They put him in a juvenile facility. Not great, but not too bad.

The man, though, got hard time.

I felt sorry for him. Sure, what he did shouldn't have been done. Fine. But people on the outside generally don't know what happens to a guy who goes in. They especially don't know what happens to a guy who goes in for doing something to a kid. Sure, there are television shows that advertise how they show the truth of life behind bars. They can't, though. There is no way to really show it.

Especially what happens to guys who have sex with kids.

I wasn't in with the guy I'm talking about, but I've been in. I've done time. I saw a different guy. His thing was little girls. He'd done some pretty messed up things with a few of them. Somehow, people found out after he was put inside.

That happens. Guards talk to guys doing clean up detail. Guys hoping to get out early by kissing ass, sometimes literally. Those guys talk to guys who aren't so cooperative. Those guys talk to other guys. Pretty soon, even the guys in solitary know.

I was only around one time to see what they did to him. I'll never forget it, though. See, when I'm doing what I do, I have my game face on. You have to. You don't really feel much. It's been that way for me for a long time. Inside, though, I didn't. You try to keep it on, but you just can't. Not twenty-four-seven. It doesn't work.

A group of a few guys got it all fixed up so that they'd get the same clean up detail as the guy I'm talking about. I was just nearby. These guys all had families on the outside, you see. A few had little girls about the same age as the ones he'd gotten friendly with.

They surrounded him. I could see it in his eyes. It was almost like relief. Like he'd been waiting for it. To get it over with, or something. I could kind of understand.

It started with insults. A few of the guys spit on him. Not that big a deal. It happens. Then they started hitting him. I didn't get too distracted by that. Again, it happens. When he went down on his hands and knees, they didn't stop.

He wasn't exactly a young guy, but he wasn't all that old. He didn't really make a whole lot of sound. They didn't stop, though. By this time, I'd stopped what I was doing to watch. What else was I going to do?

Once he was nearly unconscious, they hauled him up on his feet. They dragged him over to a spot on the wall where some pipes came out. One of them had somehow gotten a rope. It looked like a bunch of underwear all tied together. They tied his hands up over his head to the pipe.

Then they started beating him again. There was a lot of blood.

This wasn't all that bad, though. I'd done worse. Since then, I've done worse.

Still, there was something about it that was horrible. I guess it was because the whole time, the guy never made any noise beyond the sound of air escaping him from each blow.

Then they stripped him off and went at him with the broom handles.

At that point, I walked away. I knew he wasn't going to live through this. That, somehow, it wasn't going to be broken up in time. That no report of it would ever make it to anyone's desk.

As I walked out, though, his eyes caught mine. He was crying and, when he saw me leave, he must've realized just what I'd decided. He must've let himself believe it, too. This wasn't just going to be another beating and rape. His eyes said he knew he wasn't coming out of that room ever again.

Something about that broke something inside me, I guess. A few of the books I took from the Professor were by people who'd survived concentration camps in World War II. They say the same thing; seeing a grown man realize that he is powerless to stop his own death is nearly the most horrible moment anyone can witness.

When they sentenced that other guy from down south to go to jail, I knew he wasn't coming back out. That's just the way that is.

The kid did come out, though. I'd kept tabs on him over the years. While he'd been in, he'd learned a lot about human nature, too. I found that out when I went to his apartment and knocked on the door not long after he got out. He was just nineteen, then.

We talked. It took no time to figure out that he had no real desire to return to what the people on parole boards call, 'productive society'. It took less time to figure out what kind of sex he was looking for. So, we changed his name, Mason set up an account for him, and I showed him how to do shit.

It was the worst mistake I ever made. I swore I'd never repeat it.

We named him James Paris.

We called him Jimmy.

53 • Easy

I T'S A FIELD. Of course it's a field. I know that before I even get there.
I remember the first time I sat down in the grass.
My mother.
I haven't thought about her for a long time.

In this business, you kind of don't think about the things that make you happy. That would take away from your ability to do what you have to do. I know some guys who have wives, kids. I don't. I can't.

My mother sat in front of me. Between us was this flower. This one little fucking flower. I was young. I remember as it danced in the wind, I danced with it. My mom did, too. Only, like most adults, she couldn't become the flower. She could only imitate it.

Thing is, I was that flower.

For a few moments, I felt the sun. I moved with the wind. I was that flower.

I don't remember much else from that time. Him. Mostly, I just remember him. Yelling, slapping, kicking, punching. She never once tried to defend herself. It was just like in all those stupid movies. The ones where your stomach tenses up and you ball your fists and you're screaming in your head 'hit him back hit him back hit him back hit him back' only, they never do. Never.

I would do things to make him angry on purpose. If he wore himself out on me, he'd pass out on the floor and leave her alone. Me, I'd get better. Every time he hit her, though, she went further away.

I was little when I stopped letting her clean me up after. She'd try, and I'd kiss her and ask her to go away.

No mother should have to watch her son become what I was becoming.

The picture of the flower in my head is always followed by the sounds of the shovel. I buried her deep while he raged and screamed and threatened.

She deserved to have someone who loved her take care of that. Not some stranger.

Not him.

When I left that night, I didn't go back for years. When I did go back, he was fat, and bald. The spare key was still under the doormat. The lights were off and the place smelled like rot. He was passed out on the floor.

I tapped him on the forehead with my boot. Up to the moment he opened his eyes, I thought I'd just off him and walk away. But when I saw his iris stop down a notch as he recognized me, something came loose. Something old and vicious with years of stored poison.

"Wake up," I said.

He didn't say anything. He struggled to get up. I put my hand behind his head and shoved him up.

"You—," he said.

I sat down on the ledge in front of the fireplace. Where he used to do those things. I picked up the poker. It was still exactly where he'd always kept it. I put it on my knees, just like he always had.

"Me," I said.

He put his arms behind him and tried to stand. I grabbed the poker and smacked his elbow. He fell back to the floor. I put it back on my knees.

"Sit down," I said.

His eyes got wide.

I took my jacket off the exact same way he used to. Right arm first. Then left arm. I set it down next to me. He was just staring. It was like something out of a movie.

"What are you going to do?" he asked.

I just looked at him for a minute or two. I guess I was trying to find out if there was anything left behind his eyes. Anything at all to stop me from what I was about to do.

There wasn't.

I pulled out Wolf and asked him the same question he'd always asked me.

"Hard or easy."

He got what was about to happen. I could see it on his face. I wondered if he would remember.

"Easy?" he asked, trying not to look relieved.

He didn't remember.

Anytime I'd ever said 'easy' instead of hard, he'd used the leather strap instead of just his hand.

I picked up Wolf and pulled the hammer back. He let out a little moan. "Open your mouth," I said.

He didn't move.

I grabbed him by the back of the head and shoved him forward until Wolf was resting against his lips. He was pursing them closed, his eyes squeezed shut. I leaned in close. "Open your mouth," I whispered.

He opened his mouth and I slid Wolf in.

"Close your lips around it," I said.

He remembered, now. He remembered exactly how this had always gone. He closed his lips tight around the barrel.

"Do you remember?" I asked, staying close to his ear. He nodded his head, and I could hear him stifle back a sob. "Shhh," I said, "Don't cry. You're daddy's good little boy," I said. I leaned away and pulled the trigger.

When I drove away from the house that night, I turned the radio off and rolled down the window. I did that a lot back then. People who watched me drive by probably wondered what I was thinking, just like this movie I watched once.

There are lots of movies about what I do. Some of them good. Some bad. This one has a guy who has stumbled onto the way of the samurai. It's a pretty good movie. The guy's always looking at things.

I do that, too. I think a lot of people who watch that movie will try to guess what he's thinking about when he's quiet like that. I know, though. He's not thinking anything. That's what gets people into trouble.

Seeing. That's hard to do. Really seeing. The professor showed me lots of examples of how you see only what you want to see if you're still thinking. The Zen Buddhists, that's what they work for. Stop thinking.

If they made a bumper sticker to hand out at the meetings for the union, if there was one, it would say this: Stop thinking; it'll be the death of you. Some guys would laugh. Those are the ones who won't last the month out before they manage to die badly. Others would just stare at it. Those are the guys who are just starting to really see. Other guys would smile a little and nod without saying anything.

The movie was good, though. The guy was really clever. Problem with samurai is this; they are tied to a master. Essential problem of mankind, the professor said. How do you live without serving? That singer from the sixties said it best when he said 'Everybody's got to serve somebody'.

I guess I serve Mason. He's not my master. He was just the guy that gave me a place to stay when I was younger. He was the one who introduced me to Emmaus.

No way around it, though.

I have to kill him.

54 • Questions

I REMEMBER A few years back some guy got nailed for writing a book about what I do. That's nothing new. Those have been around for a long long time. Emmaus had a few that he'd learned from as a new guy. The problem was that the guy who used it had left it sitting around after one of his hits. That was stupid.

If there was a union, they'd be against these books. Too easy. Anyone can pick one up, read a chapter and then make business cards for himself that say 'Problems solved'. They start wearing leather duster jackets and calling themselves 'Ice' or whatever. I hear a lot of Eastern religions have this problem, too.

I didn't read the one he used, but obviously there was a problem with it. It didn't have a section marked 'burn this book when you've learned everything'. That's true with a lot of books, but especially these.

So, the mark's family finds the book, and presses charges. They can't get the guy who did their husband/dad/uncle, etc. But, what they can do, is get the guy who published the book. They try this all the time. That Russian guy with the book about the little girl? They tried it with him.

It's funny that people so dependant on books are so afraid of what's in them.

I'm thinking this as the car drones on and on.

Dubois isn't moving in the seat next to me. The clock on the dashboard says eleven thirty. Almost time.

"So," he says after a while, "where are we going?"

"She said I'd know," I say.

He waits. He's looking at me, so I know he wants to ask more. He looks away at the road, then turns back, "How?"

"I don't know."

"Then how can you—"

"I said, I don't know."

He gets quiet. He adjusts himself in the seat. I can tell he's uncomfortable. I almost want to apologize. I remember how that felt; that soreness that won't go away, but only gets worse with each movement.

"Slouch down so that your ass hangs off the seat," I say.

He looks at me for a second, then slides down. Almost immediately, his face relaxes. He closes his eyes.

"What did he do?" I ask. I don't know why I ask, but I do.

"Who?"

"You know who," I say.

"Oh," he says. The quiet spins out between us again, and I wonder if it is the break in the conversation, or if the conversation is the break in it.

"I guess he likes to cut people up," he says, "He was touching himself while he got the tools and shit ready." His voice is droning. He's in that other place. I can tell.

A reflective green sign passes. It reads 'Yeats Preserve: 15 MI'.

That's it. I don't know how I know, I just do.

DuBois isn't saying anything anymore. He's just staring ahead. I reach down and set the trip meter to zero.

"What's that?" he asks.

"She's at the Preserve. That's where she's got Gan," I say.

"How do you know that?" he asks.

I turn my head to look at him. He nods, then looks back at the road.

"So how did you know what to do?" he asks.

"With what?"

"You know; how to sit."

For a second, I think about explaining to him. I wonder why. That's when it hits me. I've never told anyone. About Emmaus or any of it. Even the Professor. He didn't ask, so I didn't say. I was too busy listening.

"I used to be one of Mason's boys," I say.

He sits up without thinking, then winces. A part of me is happy to get that much of a reaction. He slides back down, still looking at me.

"When?"

I turn to him, "You ask a lot of questions."

"That's generally how most of us here in the real world get information; When?"

"I was young. Fifteen, maybe."

I could tell that was sinking in. He went quiet again. That settled it.

"You didn't get cut up or anything?"

"One of the first guys took a liking to me. I got lucky."

"Oh," was all he said.

Up ahead on the right, I could see some cars. The trip meter said ten, so this wasn't the preserve. Blue sign passed on the right that said 'Rest Area'.

"Could we pull in?" he asked.

"For what?"

"I have to go."

I exhale and pull the car onto the small road, twisting through the large diesel parking lots to the small building nestled in trees. I left the car running and hit the button to unlock the door. He sat up carefully, then got out. I watched him go inside.

To most gay men, DuBois would be attractive. I noticed him moving. I thought about whether or not most people notice how the other people in their life move. DuBois moved with his fingers loose. His shoulders moved with his hips. I wondered what I looked like when I moved.

Rest area. They're the same everywhere. No matter where you go, it's the same thing. Even as I thought that, though, I knew it wasn't right. There'd be differences. Across the way, I watch as some kid plows over the curb. Too fast on the road leading from the highway. He gets out screaming. He's got the tire off already, when I look up and notice that DuBois isn't back yet.

I shut the car off and get out. Thick air. Cold. I walk up the path to the restroom. It's called lots of things in lots of places. Why rest room here, I'll never know.

Inside, I already know what's going on. Only one stall is closed, and two sets of tennis shoes show underneath the door. Facing each other. Slurping sounds. I start to piss. Startled sounds. The stall door opens and the man I'd just seen pull in with a station wagon, three kids and a wife in tow, leaves quickly. DuBois comes out wiping his mouth.

I look at him.

"What?" he asks, cheeks turning red.

I finish, flush, and zip up. I go to the sink and run hot water. He's watching me in the mirror.

"What am I supposed to do when you find this kid? I need money."

I look up at him in the mirror, then shut the faucet off. Dry my hands with paper towels. Walk out.

He follows to the car.

"Is there going to be an after?" he asks, flopping into the seat and closing the door. I start the car, turn the air conditioning on.

"I don't know."

"So there may not be?" he asks.

"You knew that already," I say.

He nods to himself. He knew already.

I pull out of the rest area and onto the highway again.

Zeus was king of the gods. That's why I picked the name. Thunder. A warrior's name was a source of power and strength. It was a way for the warrior to call on the spirit of the animal he was named for. A connection between them.

Only, I'm not feeling very powerful anymore. She's got me. She can ask for anything she wants, and she knows that. Meeting Gan and I just one time was enough to tell her that. And then she challenged me.

Where did that power go?

Thinking about her brings me almost to the point. My hands are white gripping the wheel. She was graceful, like a bird, almost. She was unafraid of the raw strength that got me so far with everyone else.

I used to be a god. If I can be challenged, then I'm not one anymore.

If I'm not a god, anymore, what am I?

55 • Dharma Dueling

ONCE KNEW this guy named Creed. Tough guy. Worked for one of Mason's associates. Mostly in money collection. We were at this bar.

He said to me that getting money from rich people was way harder. I asked him how he figured that and he told me "Easy. Poor people is stupid. They don't know how to play games wit you."

I wondered if that was true for a second, then I said "That's not true."

"How you figure?" he asked.

"The guys I go see, they've been huffing it for years. Since they were kids they been crooked," I said.

"So?"

"Guys you see, they're crooked, but it's new to them. They know some stuff. But it's something they switch on switch off."

"What the fuck does that mean?" he asked.

"Guys I see, they *are* crooked. They don't turn it on. They're not acting bent; they just are."

He sat back in his chair after I said that. Puffed some. You could hear the gears turning.

There were these masters of Buddhism. Used to go around and meet up with each other and talk about the truth. Dharma, they called it. Professor had a book by a guy that had that in the title. I remember I liked that book.

But these masters would sit and quiz each other. Talk about truth and reality. Problem is, way I see it? If they're so enlightened, why does one have to be right and one wrong?

How does an enlightened person still have an ego to feed?

I paid the bill and walked out.

He got aced a few weeks later. Some junkie kid, I heard.

56 • The Note

THERE'S A LINE to get into the Preserve. Some sort of tourist attraction.

Giant cardboard signs that look like Swans. That's the big attraction of the park: The Swans. All kinds of birds, but the swans in particular.

In the line, DuBois can't hold still.

"What?" I ask.

"Nothing," he says. He doesn't stop moving.

Two spots in line ahead of us, there is a woman and her little girl. They look exactly alike, down to the berets. That has to be on purpose. The little girl is full of questions. I think about Gan, and how he never was. I look over at DuBois again.

He's rubbing one arm with the other.

"Mommy, are swans powerful?" the little girl asks. Her mother doesn't answer and I wonder why. It's a legitimate question.

"What is it?" I ask. DuBois moving around is like a strobe light in my peripheral.

"Nothing. I just can't hold still."

"Mommy, can swans and people have babies?"

"No, Helen, now please be quiet for a minute," The mother says.

"Silly kid," DuBois says, under his breath. Problem is, like most people, he doesn't understand just how loud his whisper is. I wonder if, in some way, he's hoping that the little girl would hear. She does hear, and looks up at us.

Instead of looking away, she smiles at me. Millions of tax dollars spent on 'Stranger Danger' education in schools down the drain. She starts to play, but always looking out of the corner of her eye to make sure I'm watching. She's got this little glass wall. I wonder what sort of toy that is. A wall. A glass replica of a wall.

"What's so silly about that question?" I ask DuBois.

He just looks at me.

Something shatters. I snap my head around. The little girl has dropped something made of glass.

"Mommy, mommy, I broke my wall!" She says, panicky.

"Helen, goddammit. Why do you always have to be so willful and destructive?" the mother asks. The little girl is in tears. They are next to purchase tickets, so the mess gets left behind.

When DuBois and I get to the ticket window, a boy, face covered in pimples, steps back from me. He's behind glass, but still steps back.

"Whoa," is all he can manage, like some kid from a sitcom.

"What?" I ask. I can see myself in the reflection. I'm not doing more than default menacing. He shouldn't be more than mildly uncomfortable.

"Nothing. Just. Whoa," he says again, reaching under the desk for something. I'm wondering if I'm going to have to shoot him. I'm running through pictures in my head to see if maybe I should know him from somewhere. My hand is creeping toward Wolf.

He comes back up with an envelope in his hand.

On the front it says 'Zeus' in hurried blue ink.

"She described you," the boy says, shoving the envelope through a slot at the bottom of the window.

I open it. It smells like her.

"I'm not in Yeats. Neither is Ganymede."

I put the note back in the envelope. I put the envelope in my pocket. I step out of line.

"What did it say?" DuBois asks.

"She's doesn't have him here," I say.

"But she said you'd know," DuBois says.

I don't say anything. Out in the parking lot, a large blue truck is pulling up next to my car. One of those old Dustbowl deals. Truck cab, back made into a flat bed with high wooden sides. There is a sign on the side of it, but I can't read it.

A man gets out. Dirty clothes. Beat up hat. He beats it on his jeans, then puts it back on. The dust makes a cloud around him. He walks toward the line.

I move around a bit to see if I can read the sign. Something about it catches my attention. Just as the man passes, I see the sign. Black with big white letters: 'Chuck P.'s Sheep farm'. It's written all curly and puffy, to remind you of wool.

He walks right up to the glass without attempting to get in the line. In the booth, some girl, dressed in the same tie and vest as the boy, is putting her purse on the desk as the boy is standing up.

I clear my throat.

He turn around "Yah?"

I point back at his truck, "How far?"

The nametag sewn into his blue shirt says 'Ellis'. I wonder if that's his last name. If he got kidded in grade school about it sounding like 'Elvis'.

"Bout tree mile up ta road," he says, already turning back around. He looks a lot like the kid. Father, uncle maybe.

I turn around and walk to the car.

"Is that where she is?" DuBois asks.

"Yes," I say. I get it, now.

"How do you know?" he asks.

I swing into the seat and close the door in one motion. It all clicks into place in my head.

I remember at the end of that movie. The one about the black hitman obsessed with being a Samurai. He left his book behind.

The last thing that is shown is the little girl reading the book. The Professor once told me that books represent power. It's a symbol, he said. I guess that scene is supposed to show that the power has been given to her.

It's a fucked up way to end a movie.

57 • Dissecting Murder

OST OF THE guys who used to do stuff to me wanted to go to the movies. I guess that's some fantasy. Take a kid to the movies and put your hand in his pocket or whatever.

I didn't mind so much. I liked movies. One of my favorite things was when someone wanted to go to one of those art theaters. Especially if they were showing something old. I went one time and watched 'Frankenstein'.

I liked the movie a lot.

The Professor told me about the book all those years later and I wondered why it was that they didn't make the movie like the book. The book sounded better. When I read it, it was better. The Professor told me about this quote from some dead poet who said that people kill things to open them up and see what's going on. We murder to cut open or dissect or something like that. I thought, that's really true. We murder to dissect. That's it. That's what he said.

I wondered if there was a way to find out how something works without killing it.

I thought a lot about Virginia and Wolf. In that one movie about the guys going off to Vietnam, they do a chant where they hold up their rifles while they march and say "this is my rifle," then they grab their crotches and say "this is my gun." Even when I was a kid with some guys hand stuffed down my jeans, I didn't think that was right.

My guns are me. I can live without them, but they can't live without me.

The professor always talked about that poet who wrote about the wheelbarrow. About how much depends on it. I wonder if that's true. To me, so much depends on guns. I wonder when that changed.

Funny thing about a .45 is not that it kills; it's designed to do that. No, the funny thing about a .45 is that it can kill. Some people think that's what they are; killers. But they aren't. Two quick flicks of the wrist and the whole thing is just a pile of metal, some bullets and a couple of gears. Nothing without a human. But guns kill humans. Can't make more of themselves. Can't think for themselves. Just kill. But they're fragile. I wonder how many people really think about that while they're holding one.

A gun isn't power. A gun is weakness.

There's that bumper sticker "Guns don't kill people; people kill people." I wonder how many soccer moms, driving down the street really understand what that means. Just how true it is.

In ancient times, martial art master-types were said to have weird mind powers. One of the ones they talked about was the ability to kill using only their mind. If there was a union for guys like me, we'd need to have those guys come in a do one of those things. Those workshops. Some Oprah shit.

I carry guns. But Virginia, Wolf, none of them ever killed anyone. They just explode bullets. *I kill.*

I'm the one who kills.

58 • Sleeping

SOMETIMES I SLEEP. When I do, I dream. That's not unusual.

Sometimes, though, I think.

Sometimes I think maybe I'm trying to sleep in the middle of all this chaos. That I'm not alone. That, somewhere, someone is sitting in a dark room, sweating from fever, clicking my life into an outdated computer. My life feels like that. Like some novel.

Picture trying to sleep in the middle of a rock concert. Dead middle of the crowd, a little twin bed. Imagine someone coming through the crowd; no one sees him but me. He leans down and kisses my forehead while I'm sleeping.

I usually wake up just after that part.

My guns feel too close.

It makes me wonder about all the people in the Professor's books. Do they know? I mean, do they really know? The kid with the runaway slave; does he know? The woman watching her plantation burn, does she know?

I'd never tell anyone this.

Not anyone but Gan.

He asked me the same question. Turned away from the window and asked "Do you ever feel like you're just a piece on a chessboard?" What I said was no. What I did inside was 'yes' with my whole self.

He said "Sometimes, I feel like I'm on my back on this huge raft floating down a river, and I can't look up to see where I'm going, except in short little bursts. I don't like that feeling." What I wondered is, if we're just people in a book somewhere, then why are we like this?

Why did he have to take it for money? Why did I?

I didn't tell him until later, when he was asleep, about all this.

And now I'm thinking it as the car flies toward what's about to happen. And I wonder if he's cold. I wonder if he's bleeding. I wonder if he knows I'm coming, or if he's asleep and feels safe.

What I say inside is, 'if you're out there, watching over him, please let him be okay.' There isn't a response. None except black road, white dashes and the hum of wind past the windows.

It's better than nothing.

59 • Second Showdown

IT'S HOT. Dubois and me walking across the grass. The car's engine ticking itself to sleep behind us. He's not saying anything. My hand is on Virginia.

"How do you know where to look?" Dubois asks me for the thirtieth time. I don't tell him. He wouldn't understand it. It's not about knowing. It's about feeling.

People everywhere. Bright shirts, cheap sunglasses. Kids. It's always hard to see them. You wonder what's happened. If it will happen. You try not to look. By trying not to, it just happens more. I notice Dubois looking, too.

"Stop," I say. He looks at me like he's about to say something, then doesn't.

The path leads up ahead. Just over some small hills. I can see a pond. A little imitation Greek temple.

"There," I say. I can feel them. Her and Gan. Just behind the pillars of that temple.

Sheep. There are sheep everywhere. Not just the tourists. Real sheep. It's what the place is known for. Coming down the hill, there must be seventy of them eating grass. Kids petting them, rubbing their hands.

"Lanolin," Dubois says.

"What?"

"The oily stuff. Lanolin. It's in the wool. Comes off on your hands."

I don't say anything. Dubois is falling a bit behind me. I stop. He comes forward. I can tell he senses that this whole thing is drawing to a close. Him, me, Gan, all of it. For what? A bill unpaid? I'm ready for it to be over. Doesn't matter how. I might die. Whatever. If there was a union, it would be in the bylaws that you'd have to be ready to die, all day, every day. It's the job.

I want Gan to escape.

The water has a cool breeze coming off of it. I step closer. Large fish in there. I can see them moving just under the surface.

"Koi," Dubois says.

I don't answer. I look up. She's there. On the pedestal of the cheap knock off temple. She looks so beautiful. Gan stands in front of her. My insides jump for a second until I settle them. Inhale. Exhale. Black smoke coming out of me. He looks okay. Scared, too thin. Too thin.

I put my hand under Dubois' elbow. He looks down at it as if he's about to say something, then doesn't. I pull him to the right. We have to go around the pond to get to the temple.

"What's going to happen?" Dubois whispers. We're around the lake. She's got her hand under Gan's elbow on the opposite side. Her hand resting on her gun under her jacket. She's a lefty. I didn't know.

We come to a place just behind the temple. Ten feet. That's all that separates me now. She stands there, head cocked to the side. Gan is breathing hard.

"Zeus," is all she says.

"Here's Dubois," I say, but I don't let go of him.

"We can't do this here," she says

"Bullshit. This is where you wanted, this is where it happens," I say. I keep thinking to myself 'she won't kill him, she won't kill him'. Inhale. Exhale.

"Send the man over, then I let go of the boy," she says.

Inhale. Exhale. "How fucking stupid do you think I am, lady?" I ask.

She closes her eyes for a second. Inhale. Exhale. My fingers tighten on Virginia.

"I can't do anything if you're not going to trust me."

"Fuck you and your trust." I look over at Gan, "You alright?" I ask. Inhale. Exhale.

"Yeah, 'm okay," he mumbles.

"We each let go on three. One, two, three, let go, got it? No cutesy shit. I will shoot you right here, lady," I say. I'm warning her. That's not good. A dog that barks won't bite. Warnings are for pussies, that's an unofficial bylaw of the union.

"Okay," she says.

"One," I say. Inhale. Exhale.

"Two," I say. Inhale. Exhale.

"Three," I say. Inhale.

She shoves Gan at me and lunges for Dubois. I knew she was going to do that. I spin past Gan's shoulder, as if we were dancing. She's close to Dubois.

For the first time in my life I don't want to hit someone, but I can't let her get him.

I promised.

I pull the trigger. She spins around at the ankle, facing me as she falls. I pull again. She falls faster, rocketing to the ground. I follow her with the muzzle. I pull again when her head bounces. Her whole body jumps off the ground.

Blood all over Dubois. His mouth wide open. Gan on the ground, hands over ears. That's when I hear it. A screaming. Movement everywhere. I look up. Sheep. Running. People and animals, all running in any direction they can to get away from here. I look back down at Leeda.

I walk to Gan. I put my hand under his elbow. He looks up at me. I exhale.

He attaches himself to me at the waist. I close my eyes, put my arm around him. I open my eyes to Dubois. He still hasn't closed his mouth. I grab Gan's shoulder and pull him away from me. I walk to Leeda.

"Get Gan to the car. Start it. I'll be there in a minute," I say to Dubois.

He doesn't move. As I kneel down next to her, without looking at him, I say "Now." He moves. I hear their footsteps across the grass behind me.

Her eyes follow me as I crouch.

"Why sheep?" I ask.

"Please—," she whispers. That gasping breath that dying people have. She's thinking she can't believe she's been shot. I pull her gun out of her hand.

"Why sheep?" I ask again.

"Don't let—," she says. Fading.

I pull out a set of matches. I pull out a small vial I have in my pocket. I open the vial and pour it on her chest, "This'll even burn your enamel. No traces," I say.

She smiles, closes her eyes.

I put Virginia to her temple. Pull the trigger again. Then I light the match. I stand up, drop it on her. She lights instantly. Funeral pyre, just like ancient warriors.

I turn away from her. Walk to the car.

60 • Hotel

OUTSIDE, ON THE interstate, eighteen wheelers are flying by. I can hear them. That huge wind rush every two or three seconds. It sounds like some god or monster is late for something. I wonder what.

In the curtain, I can see Dubois outline. He's smoking. I didn't know he smoked. I can see each inhale. Each exhale. His arms crossed over his chest. His head tilts up with each stream of smoke he lets go. I could use a cigar. I could use some food, too. It's been a long couple of days.

The bed shifts some. Gan moves. That weird fish-move people do when sick; push head into the mattress to lift up lower back and move it left or right. He lets out a little moan. Breaths in through his mouth.

He's sleeping.

He spends a lot of time while we're together sleeping.

When he's sleeping is the only time I settle. My guns are on the long, low desk against the wall. They don't feel far, just waiting.

That same feeling you get when, as a kid, you notice the first wasp sitting upside down on it's paper nest. I refuse to follow the rest of that thought. I let it die. I reach out and touch Gan's arm. He's solid. He's real. I let myself grasp him with all my senses. It's like breathing in after a long time underwater.

"Zeus," he whispers.

"Yeah."

"Thank you."

"For what?"

"Coming to get me."

I don't know what to say to that. In silhouette on the curtain, Dubois drops one cigarette, after lighting a fresh one. Continues his puffing routine.

"You don't have to thank me."

"Yes, I do," he says, then turns over. I can't see his face all that well, but I know he's looking right at me, "Why?"

"Why what?"

"Why did you come after me."

"I told you, don't start with that gay shit."

"I'm not," he says in that voice that says he was about to.

"What kind of question is that to ask me?"

"I dunno. I just wanted to hear you say it."

Inhale. Exhale.

"Do you know that little part of you inside that likes to be touched? That part that likes to sing?"

"Sort of."

"If you," I say, then growl. A big part of me doesn't want to say this.

"What," he says, turning on his side to face me.

"That part inside everyone that's still like a little kid, you know?" I say. I can't believe I'm talking like this. It doesn't seem like me. The Professor would say that this is breaking character unity. That I'm nullifying the unspoken contract between audience and myself to remain close to constant.

"Yeah," he says.

"I can't feel that anymore."

"Oh," he says, and I can tell his eyes are closed.

"But you can," I say. This is torture. Worse, I've been tortured, and that, at least, you can just walk away from and let the body take. This I have to be here for.

"Sometimes," he says.

"They hurt you just like me, only you can still feel that part," I say.

He reaches out and touches my face. His fingers are cool, and smell just like him, "Do you want me to show you how? Is that what you mean?" he asks.

"No," I say, thinking 'here it comes', "I think—" I get to the edge, and can't do it.

"Say it," he says, putting his fingers on my lips.

"I think you are that part of me. That somehow it came loose and here you are," I say.

That's it, ladies and gentlemen. Contract broken. Please check your area to make sure no valuables have been left behind and carry your trash to the receptacles located outside. We hope you enjoyed your stay.

Only, no mad rush for the exits. He's still in bed. His fingers are still on my lips.

"Is that why you won't do anything to me? Touch me like other men have?" he asks.

"Yes," I says. I can't even think of the routine, let alone do it. My heart is gulping and screaming in my chest.

He doesn't say anything. Turns over. Puts his back against my chest. Grabs my arm, pulls it around him. Snuggles head deep into pillow. Drifts into sleep. He's always sleeping when I'm around.

Dubois had asked 'what now?' in the car. I told him I didn't know. But I do. I always do. This whole thing is coming to an end. That means that, after rescuing someone, one last monster has to be killed. I have to go do one more thing, then it's over. Then I can take Gan somewhere and be safe.

Outside, Dubois drops another cigarette, puts his hands on his hips, exhales upward, looking at the stars. People who smoke do that, make that one last impassioned look upward, then go back inside. He moves, and the sound of the doorknob clicking. He comes into the room, then closes the door. My eyes are shut but I can follow his progress through the room.

He locks the deadbolt, then walks slow to the bathroom. He closes the bathroom door and the shower starts. He'll touch himself, clean off, then fall onto the bed and into a fitless sleep. It's probably been his routine since he was in junior high school.

And I will lay here all night, listening to both of them breathe.

Holding Gan.

Knowing I have to go kill Mason.

61 • Once Dancing

I NEVER TOLD anybody then, but I looked in windows a lot. I think most kids do. Even if the windows are closed, they try. I did.

Just down from the corner I used to work, this dance studio opened up. Waiting for money to show up, I'd watch. I watched them dance. I don't tell people that because it's mine. The one thing that's really mine. I would stand there and watch them. Guys and girls. I couldn't believe that.

They were soft. Even in hard joint flexing, they seemed soft. A few times, when I was really young, and I got a chance to shower, I would ape their movements. I can't think of it as any other word. I am not a graceful person. I never have been. The first time I tried to ape them in the mirror, I discovered just what it was they were doing.

I remembered the flower, and my mother.

When they stretched arms above their heads, touching fingers, they were the sun. When they stretched hands in front as if carrying a basket, they were the world. I could feel that. Only, in the mirror, I just looked like scars.

I guess we're all meant for different things.

I watched enough that most times, when guys were doing things to me, I would repeat their whole day in my head, from warm up to cool down. The stretches, the movements. I could even imagine those movements put together in long, flowing sequences. It helped. I could come back and ignore the pain. The professor would probably call that something like 'walling myself in a place of beauty'. He'd say something about how most people who survive things do that.

That dance studio was there for a year or more. Then one day I came to the corner, and the doors were draped with yellow police tape. The windows got boarded up the next day. No one came to dance anymore.

I stopped trying to ape them in the mirror.

Eventually, the dances faded, except one image.

One of the days I was watching, an older woman who still had strong legs was walking in slow circles around this one boy. He was tall and very thin. He looked like he might break at any minute. The woman kept saying something to him, and he looked tense and hurt.

Then she stopped walking, put her hands on his shoulder and smiled. He smiled back, and she stretched up as far as she could. He mimicked her. Then she started swaying as if caught in a light breeze. He mimicked, and something caught in my chest.

Just then a guy came up with money. I had to go. But I kept that image. The flower, swaying. Dancing with that flower, once, a long time ago.

62 • Game Plan

WHAT ARE YOU going to do with the kid?" Lincoln asks.

I don't answer. The iron railing groans against my weight. I've got a few ideas. It all depends on what happens when I go see Mason.

"Do you know what you're going to do?" Lincoln asks.

"Not yet," I say.

Just beyond, the Interstate hums. Hundreds of thousands of cars go by just while we've been talking. The smoke from my cigarette drifts out from me and over them. We connect that way. I exhale.

"I didn't know you smoked."

"I usually don't."

"Why now?" Lincoln asks, leaning on the railing, too. It groans and gives just a bit. He stands back up. I smile.

"You ask a lot of questions."

He didn't say anything.

"Are you going to take him with you?"

"To where?" I ask, knowing what he means.

"You know what I mean."

I hadn't thought about it. "I hadn't thought about it," I say. Doing what I have to do to Mason is taking up all of me. It has to. This is no ordinary dragon to slay.

Lincoln puts his hand on my back. Deep down, way inside, alarms go off. I start to stiffen up my back. But then he rubs my back. Slow. I can hear the material of my shirt make that 'swish' sound.

"We could just leave. All three of us. Just leave," he says into the darkness.

"No," I say.

"Why not?"

"You don't understand Mason. Men like him. If I run, he will chase me. No," I say, "I have to kill him." Saying that out loud makes me nervous.

"I don't understand why," Lincoln says.

"You're right. You don't."

His hand stops moving. Somewhere, a voice wishes it wouldn't.

"It's about the principle. I've taken something from him."

"But you said the boy was for a client of his."

"Yeah, Gan was. But that doesn't matter. Not to a guy like Mason."

I wait.

"Did you enjoy hurting me?" Lincoln asks. His hand still on my back.

"What?" I know what he means. But I know what he wants right now. He needs to say this.

"When you came to get me. You beat me. You raped me. Did you enjoy that?"

"Do you want me to lie?" I ask.

"No."

"Then no."

"You're lying."

"Why would I?" I say. Just then a huge eighteen-wheeler rolls by. It rattles the thin concrete walkway of the second floor we're on. In the humid night, bugs swarm around the lights just outside each hotel room door.

"You didn't, then?" he asks. His hand moves a little.

"No. I didn't. It's a job. I do my job. I do it well," I say, "but I don't like it."

Quiet comes down again.

"What happens after you kill this Mason?" he asks.

"After, it doesn't matter."

"What do you mean."

"Just that. After, it doesn't matter what I do. It'll be over."

"Won't they come after you?"

If there was a union, this would be a big thing. There'd always be meetings and focus groups or whatever. In ancient Japan, a Samurai was bonded to his lord. Period. End of sentence. But there were guys who had the training, the talent, the weapons, who were not tied down. They could do whatever they wanted. They were called Ronin.

"Ronin," I say.

"What?"

"No. They won't come after me."

"How do you know?" he asks. I straighten up, turn.

"Stop asking so many questions," I say, flicking what's left of cigarette over side railing.

"But don't you think you need some sort of game plan?"

"Why?" I ask. Plans fall apart. There was a poem about that. Some Scottish guy. The professor said he was a genius before people recognized such things. If you're ready, the Buddhists say, you're ready.

Plans only get in the way.

Through the curtain, I can see Gan moving. He's awake. Whatever drugs she gave him are finally wearing off. He's been sleeping long stretches.

Mason looks off toward the Interstate. I watch Gan.

It's perfect.

63 • Loose Ends

THE ELEVATOR MOVES with a quiet hum. Upward. Seems I'm always going upward in elevators. Inhale.

I can feel the slight rattle of the box. Hear the gears turning above me. Exhale.

Inhale. I pull deep this time. Catch all the left over black smoke inside me.

Hold.

Exhale.

Through half-lidded eyes, the light comes on behind the number 34. Two more. I wonder who'll be watching him today. Probably Herman.

The last bit of black smoke leaves me as the elevator slows. Stops. Seconds of odd as the motor stops and the cord stretches, then comes back. Giant box on a rubber band. The doors ding, then part.

Small hallway. At the end, a door. Number 341. Little table halfway down the hall with a large vase. Magnolias. I pull Virginia and Wolf.

Let's get this over with.

When my foot hits the door, it explodes inward. I step through.

Just inside, the desk. No one behind it. It's after five. Knew no one would be.

To the right, the door to Mason's office. Closed.

From behind, a clicking sound. I hit the floor. Inhale. An explosion happens where my head was a second ago. I roll on my shoulder.

It's Herman. All six-foot-five, two hundred seventy pounds of Herman. With a gun. I'm pulling back both my triggers as he pulls his. Idle, my brain tries to remember what his gun is named.

The floor just in front of me explodes.

So does Herman's left shoulder.

I roll to one side of the little desk.

He rolls to the other.

This could go all night. I don't have time to play .45 caliber peek-a-boo. Mason is likely just about to step out of his office with a shotgun. He has one in there. It has to be now.

I stand up. Move a little to my right. Kick the desk to the side. Herman knew, already coming up to a crouch. I pull both triggers again. Herman's gun flashes. Herman explodes, flying backward. That's when I feel it. The searing heat. My arm.

Herman shot my arm.

It's not the first time I've ever been shot. You never forget that one. It hurts almost as bad, though. I want to scream when I try to move it. Reddish-black fills the edges of my vision when I try. Fuck.

"What in the sam hell is going on out there. Herman?" Mason is saying through his door. Not as muffled as it should be. He's managed to get all of his fat out from behind the desk. Probably already has the shotgun.

I hold my good arm out to full length and sight along Wolf. I move down the door enough. I wait. Just underneath the door, there's a space. It's pretty big. They do that in the South. Leave big spaces under doors. I see the shadows change under the door. Grey. Darker. Darker. Very dark.

I pull the trigger.

The sound he makes is almost funny. It sounds like he's more surprised than anything else. Then comes the huge 'thud'. Some crashing sounds. Through the new hole in the door, I can see the desk got moved back when he fell on it.

"Oh, lord Jesus, I'm shot. I'm shot. Oh, lord Jesus—" He keeps wailing.

He built this whole thing when he was younger. He was incredibly tough, then. Had a reputation for being crazy. He'd do anything. No fear. That kind of thing gets respect on streets.

Still holding Wolf out, cradling the other arm against me, I walk to the door.

"Who the fuck are you, you motherfucker, I will fucking—" He just keeps spitting words at me. He doesn't even know yet.

From the left side of the door, through the hole, I can see he's lost the shotgun. That's good for me. I turn to face the door. Kick the knob. The door crashes inward.

I step in. Exhale.

The look on Mason's face is indescribable. Fear, betrayal, whatever.

"You," is all he says.

I don't say anything.

"How the fuck did you get in here?" he asks.

"You've gotten lazy. You spent so long thinking no one would dare come after you. You forgot that maybe someone would."

"Fuck you. What's all this prodigal son bullshit, boy? I should kill you right now, shouldn't I though," he says, laying on his side, bleeding. I got him just below his sternum. He'll live for a while.

I pull over one of the chairs that faced his desk.

I sit down.

"This is bullshit, son. Do you know what you're doing?" he asks.

I nod. Wolf aimed at him, Virginia in my lap. My arm throbs.

"What is it you want? The boy? Shit, son, I got at least a hundred more you could have, if that's what you want. I never knew that's what you wanted, or I'd have given you the pick of the litter—"

I close my eyes. He stops talking.

"You're not in love with this one, are you?" he asks.

I don't know how to answer that. I open my eyes.

"Addresses," is all I say.

"Are you hopped up on something, boy?" he asks. He's trying to get power back in this situation. I've seen this before. If we had a union, one of the things they'd teach us about is how people act when they have a gun pointed at them.

"I want the addresses. Where are they now, where you got them from. All of them."

He doesn't say anything for a moment. Then, "Are you fucking kidding me son?"

I shoot him in the leg.

He screams, writhes. The look on his face isn't pain, though. It's embarrassment.

"Quiet," I say. He tries. Like a little kid told to stop crying with a threat.

"I want the address book. The phone numbers. The contacts. The others like Paris," I say. His eyes get wide. He didn't know I remembered about Paris.

He's bleeding. I can see his mind work. He knows he doesn't have a lot of time. I've been through this before. He's going to offer me something else. He's going to try to get control back.

"Now, boy, put down that hog-leg, and let's talk some sense."

"No. I won't," I said. The gun still pointed at his chest.

"Have you lost your gawd dammed mind, son?"

"For the first time in a long time, I know exactly what I'm doing."

"*Do* you realize what you're doing, hyah, boy?" he asked.

"Yes."

"Did I evah once play you wrong, boy?" he asks. I knew he would.

"No."

"When I took you in, boy, you were nothin'. A beat up little runt suckin' cock for enough money to get a hotdog a day. Weren't you just," he says.

I don't say anything.

"This is the thanks I get?" he asks, "the thanks for taking you in, not selling you off?"

"I want the address book. The phone numbers. The contacts."

"I sent Emmaus over to you. Thought you were the one he was lookin' for."

"Give me the book," I say.

"He took you and gave you a gun. Gave you confidence, boy. And look at you now."

"There are more bullets in this gun," I say.

He stops, looks at me. "Do you realize what you're doing, boy?"

"Yes. I do. The book. Where is it?"

"You can't, son. You can't possibly imagine."

"For twenty years, now, I have done what you asked. The shit you couldn't bring yourself to do anymore. I know exactly who you are, who you deal with, and what you're capable of. I know exactly what I'm doing," I say.

"Then you know that there is nowhere you will be able to go, nowhere you will be able to hide, boy," he spat.

"I know. I won't be able to stay anywhere in America, or Europe, not even Mexico."

"You're gawd dammed right you won't, son."

"You're stalling for time," I said.

He looked at me without speaking.

"All marks stall for time. Only, not all marks have a silent alarm system underneath their desks. I suppose you're waiting on Herman to come busting in here," I say.

He's still just looking at me.

"I met Herman on the way in. Nice guy," I say.

"Alright, son, you don't have to go through the whole 'I'm a bad man' routine. I know who you are," he said. I nodded.

"So, why are you waiting, then?" he asked. Finally.

"How many right now?" I ask.

"How many what, boy?" he asks.

"I don't have to kill you, Mason. We can make this last as long as I want," I say.

He pauses, as if thinking about all the malicious things he knows Emmaus taught me, then says "Thirteen, with one supposed to be delivered next week."

"Girls or boys?" I ask.

He laughed. His belly shook, "Do you mean to tell me, boy, that you only want to help one or the other? That's a mighty picky way to save the world."

I pull the trigger. A hole appears in his left shoulder. The chair slams against the back wall. Pictures and plaques fall. The stuffed deer swings menacingly. His hand flies to the wound. His color changes.

"Girls or boys?" I ask.

"Boys! You know that, you dirty sumbitch! Boys only!" he grunts through the pain.

"Where?" I ask.

He's busy looking at his shoulder. He doesn't seem to hear me. I pull the trigger again, leaving a gaping hole in his left hand. He screams like a little girl. I should be enjoying this on some level, but I'm not. I'm past that. This is just faster than talking.

"Top drawer," he gasps, unable to drawl. He motions with his head to a small desk against the window. I walk to it, Wolf still pointing at him. Slide the drawer open. In it, a black book. I pick it up. Inside, small lines, black ink. Names, addresses. I close the book.

He's just sitting in his chair. Fat. In shock, I can tell by his color.

"You will pay, son," he whispers, through the pain.

"I know," I say. I pull the trigger once more. Then again. Then again.

"I know," I say. Turn. Walk out of the office.

64 • Walking

LINCOLN'S WAITING. The car is off. He's watching us in the mirror, trying to look like he's not.

"But I don't want to," Gan says. He's crying. Trying to hold it in. He thinks he's being brave.

"I'm sorry," I say. Behind Gan is a large building. A house. Some people I know. Good people. Some of the few.

"Why can't I come with you?" Gan asks.

"I can't take the chance that someone will take you from me again."

He bows his head down. Thinks about it some. Stifles a loud sob.

"When will I get to see you again?"

I don't say anything.

On the porch, two people standing. Old. That's how I know I can trust them. I've watched them my whole life. Never anything that tripped my suspicion.

"Get him to tell you about the wolf."

"The what?" Gan asks.

"The wolf. Ask him to tell you about the wolf. He'll know."

A pause, "but what if you die?"

"You'll be safe."

"But I don't want to be safe," he says, pouting.

He opens up his arms and latches onto me. I pull my arms up out of his, then put them around his back. I close my eyes. Feel complete for the first time ever. He's crying on me. I don't mind.

The old woman is here. She puts her hand on Gan's shoulder.

"Come along, dear," she says. Just like something from a fifties television show. That's how I know this is perfect.

He latches on harder. She smiles at me. I bend my head down, kiss the top of his.

"I have to go," I say.

He lets go slowly. Wipes his eye. Lets the old woman pull him back from me. She puts her arm around his shoulders. He lets her turn him away. I wait.

At the top of the steps, just before going inside, he stops. Turns to look at me. He turns back and walks through the door. It closes, the screen door banging shut just after.

"All that to have two weeks with him, then just take him to some old couple you know and drop him off?" Dubois says. The room is still heavy with shower mist. It smells like a hotel room, the hum of the wall unit air conditioner. Dubois is in bed, covers pulled up to make himself a cocoon. He sleeps like that. Naked, cocooned.

I'm in a chair near the round table in the room, my feet propped up on another one. Cigar smoke drifts upward. Dubois is mostly asleep; that's when he asks direct questions like that.

"You wouldn't understand."

He doesn't say anything back. On the table is the black book. A few already taken care of. More to go. I adjust my feet to get comfortable. Run down the list again. Not much longer and this all might get done.

There was that guy who wrote the book about this clam digger who goes on to become a millionaire. The professor really loved that book. It was the last one we talked about before he looked me in the face and said 'Ok'. That book ended with the last line about how we're all boats, swimming and swimming against the tide.

That's a good point to make.

When we talked about that book, he said they'd made a movie. Had some Hollywood looker-type as the main character. He said it was a fairly okay movie because they used the book. Used how people in the book talked.

People in books talk better than people in movies, he said.

In movies, they don't talk like real people. I agree with that. They talk better than real people. Movies about guys like me always have some guy in them who talks in phrases. "Shit happens" he says when his mother dies. "No one ever said life was fair" he says when the little kid's dog gets run over or whatever. Thing is, no one really talks like that. Short little sentences that are supposed to explain the world.

But from watching so many movies, everyone thinks that they have to. So people try. Guys packed in gyms start saying things like "feel the burn."

Problem is, there's no way to explain the world no matter how many words you use. The Professor says there's a guy who wrote novels that were a thousand pages with no breaks, and they still fell short. Says there were other guys who wrote books with sentences only two or three words long, and that didn't work either.

I'm thinking, if guys like that couldn't do it, then why are the rest of us trying?

65 • Epilogue II

I LOOK OVER at the passenger seat. Lincoln's been dead for over a year now, but I still look for him from time to time. Wonder if he'd still be alive if maybe I'd have been the one to go in the back door instead of him that night. It's been quiet, something I used to like, but not so much anymore.

Out the window, he's grown a lot. Gotten rangy; that mix between ragged and ready for action. Even standing next to the other kids out on the quad, he is different, focused.

Gan moves away from the group and starts up the road. The little group he was just with drift aimlessly once he's gone. I knew that's how it'd be. I spend a few more minutes just watching him, then pull out of the parking lot. I've been watching him for a few days, now. I know where he's going.

The engine rumbles to a stop once I shut the car off. For the last week, he comes here every day after he gets out of his last class. He talks to the clerk behind the counter and then walks out with a movie. I know the old man died about two years ago. I wasn't able to make the funeral—Lincoln and I were in Canada.

He comes around the corner and heads for the door. He sees the ancient black Camaro but doesn't see me inside. He's gotten dream-headed and slow. That makes me smile. He's been taken care of.

I burned the black book a month ago out in Washington. The last name crossed off. He was one of those Crowley guys; Golden Dawn, that stuff. He'd gotten it all wrong, though, and was killing the boys as sacrifices. I wonder if the police got the irony of finding him on his own altar in that position. Probably not.

As Gan comes out of the store, I open the door and step out, too.

He stops, his face a question mark.

I take my sunglasses off.

He runs to me. He slows down before he gets his arms around me and catches himself. I nod.

"It's done," I say. He puts his arms around me and buries his head in my chest. He's gotten as tall as I am, and I realize I've been away too long.

"It's done."